ENCHANTED EMPORIUM

3

Enchanted Emporium is published by Capstone Young Readers
A Capstone imprint
1710 Roe Crest Drive
North Mankato, Minnesota 56003
www.capstoneyoungreaders.com

First published in the United States in 2015 by Capstone

© 2013 Atlantyca Dreamfarm s.r.l., Italy
© 2015 for this book in English language (Capstone Young Readers)
Text by Pierdomenico Baccalario
Illustrations by Iacopo Bruno
Translated by Nanette McGuinness
Original edition published by Edizioni Piemme S.p.A., Italy
Original title: La mappa dei passaggi

Cataloging-in-Publication Data is available on the Library of Congress website.
ISBN: 978-1-4342-6518-0 (library binding)
ISBN: 978-1-62370-204-5 (paper-over-board)

Summary: The evil Semueld Askell, concealed by the Cloak of Mirrors, sneaks
into Finley's room to steal the key to the Enchanted Emporium. He discovers
that the key must be given willingly, and Finley's not about to abandon his
role as Defender of the Emporium. So Semueld forces Finley to make a terrible
choice: give him the key, or he'll make sure that Aiby Lily is lost forever.
Finley will have to use every trick in the book (as well as some magical
objects) to save his best friend.

Designer: Alison Thiele

Printed in China.
092014   008472RRDS15

MAP OF THE PASSAGES

by Pierdomenico Baccalario · Illustrations by Iacopo Bruno

CAPSTONE YOUNG READERS
a capstone imprint

TABLE OF CONTENTS

Chapter
ONE

SPARKS, TORCHES, & A BONFIRE

My father, my brother, and I headed to old lady Cumai's funeral. It was nearly dusk when we reached the top of the hill. Long clouds were shooting across the horizon like arrows without a target. Like the line of men emerging from the village, too. All of the men — and only the men.

We were all dressed in black. Since I didn't have any black clothing, my mom altered one of my grandfather's suits to fit me. She made me stand with my arms and legs spread wide so she could measure me and stick pins in the fabric. She hemmed it with white thread as a test run before sewing the real hem. She said, "Be still, Finley!" at least a hundred times, and I tried to — I really did. But I'd

never been any good at staying still. My nose suddenly itched. My knees creaked. My toes tingled. And I longed to jump, run, pedal, climb, throw a rock, or run away — anything but stand still. Even in school I was constantly restless. It's probably the reason I failed the last semester.

As my mom poked and prodded and pulled at my grandfather's suit, I prayed that the agony of altering would be over soon. "It's not my fault I can't stay still," I told her. "Patches keeps jumping on me."

Patches, my faithful adventuring companion (and scapegoat), looked up with his watery eyes from under the couch where he was resting. My mom tugged me away from him — and a little closer to the light.

It had gone on like that for two hours. Me fidgeting, my mother scolding. But as I climbed to the top of the hill with my dad and my brother, I decided it was kind of cool that we were all dressed in black. There was something important and ancient about it.

When we arrived at the top of the hill, Reverend Prospero had his back to the sea. He was muttering some psalm while two farmers stooped over the *tein-eigin*, a tool we would use to light the pyre. It was the first time I'd seen one. Well, the first time I'd seen one actually being used.

The tein-eigin is a board made of new oak with a hole in the middle. You spin a drill into the hole, also made of oak, and it begins to shoot sparks.

I watched the two men prepare the tool from behind my father's back. He seemed larger than ever in his black jacket, like one of those heroes whose deeds you read about in books while the winter wind blows or the sea roars ominously in the background.

Old lady Cumai had requested the bonfire on the hill for her funeral. She must have spoken about it with Reverend Prospero in person, or perhaps with Frankie del Latte? I couldn't imagine either scenario. Cumai had always been a mystery to me, just like the old mill that had been her home (which looked nothing like a mill). She was an eccentric woman with large blue eyes and a long neck like a daisy stem. I said hello to her every once in a while when I went fishing, but I never really spoke to her in all my thirteen and a half years. Now I was sorry for that. It's a terrible feeling to go to the funeral of someone whose voice you can't even remember.

I followed my father's lead and stood in the circle around the unlit bonfire with the other men. "Did you check to make sure you don't have any iron in your pockets?" my father asked me.

I nodded. His mood was as black as his clothing. It wasn't the first funeral we'd gone to together, and it wouldn't be the last, but it was without a doubt the strangest one.

It was one of those typical Scottish moments. You couldn't help using the word "magic" to describe the behavior of the men and our surroundings. The sea wind cut sharply across the top of the hill, shrieking as it rose along our backs below the rocky mountain peaks. The many islands in the bay stood out of the water like mysterious pyramids, seemingly waiting for something to happen. On the faces of the other men, I saw the same deep sadness that had caught hold of my father. Mr. McStay, Professor Everett, McBlack from Scary Villa — they all had a hard time looking at each other. Seamus Santangelo, the TV antenna installer, was also there. So was the Wild Thresher, and even Michael Fionnbhurd, the pub boy, whom I'd never before seen outside the pub. His pants were so short that his calves were bare, but there he was, next to the rest of us. Beside him were the baritones from the Island Choir and Jules the postman.

Jules came over to greet us as soon as he saw me. He was holding his hat in his hands as if to apologize, yet again, for when he had almost run me over with his postal van.

"Hello, Mr. Camas," he whispered to my father. "Hey, kids."

"Hi, Jules," Doug answered, patting Jules on the shoulder. "Got any mail for me?"

My brother's sense of humor was weird like that — cracking jokes at a funeral. But Jules smiled all the same. Then he looked at me uncertainly, the way someone does when they think they're seeing a ghost.

I shook Jules's hand firmly to convince him that it was really me and that I hadn't died in the accident on the coastal road. "I finally got around to writing a will," I said to him.

I'd meant it as a joke, but Jules's eyes widened in astonishment. "You, too?"

That's when I realized the experience had affected Jules as much as me. I nodded, and Jules left to take his place at the pyre.

The stack of wood in the center of our circle was a twelve-foot-tall pile of oak branches placed on a bunch of straw, broom, and heather. As I began to ask my father about the pyre, Reverend Prospero motioned for me to shut my mouth.

We waited in silence for the sun to set.

Chapter
TWO

SIGNS,
STONES, &
THE NIGHT

Time passed slowly. When the sun finally began to dip below the sea, a strange murmuring spread through the circle of men. They were watching two figures struggle up the stone path. The moment I recognized them, my heart jumped into my throat. It was Aiby Lily and her father, the owners of the Enchanted Emporium.

I thought I saw Reverend Prospero mouth a silent prayer as Locan Lily limped closer, held up by his daughter with difficulty. The two made slow, painful progress due to the nasty gunshot wound Mr. Lily was still recovering from. Across the fire, Mr. McBlack turned even paler than normal — probably because he was the one who'd accidentally shot Mr. Lily.

"What are you waiting for, you third-rate gentlemen!"

Reverend Prospero boomed, pointing at Aiby and her father. "Do you really expect a little girl to carry Locan all the way up to the top by herself?"

Doug was faster than I was — he ran over and offered his broad back as a support for Mr. Lily's other arm. Mr. Everett did the same on the other side, taking Aiby's position. They were the only two to leave their positions in the circle. The rest of the men shuffled their feet in the grass, barely hiding their annoyance at the latest arrivals.

In my foolishness, I figured their irritation was just standard Scottish mistrust. But as my brother and Mr. Everett accompanied Locan to the bonfire, I realized there was something else annoying the other men. It wasn't Mr. Lily who made them grit their teeth — it was Aiby. She was the only woman present at the funeral.

What that meant, I didn't know, but I knew there had to be a reason for the rule. I also knew I'd never find the courage to ask anyone about it because there would be no point. Scottish traditions are steeped in mystery.

I gazed over at Aiby. She looked both proud and afraid at the same time — as if she somehow knew she'd violated an unwritten rule. Or a rule written in a dead language, though Aiby always insisted that no languages were dead.

I looked out at the sea, which was turning into a melded quilt of colors. I never thought I'd see Aiby and her father at a Scottish funeral. To my embarrassment, I suppose I still sort of saw the Lilys as outsiders, too. As a matter of fact, none of us had taken the trouble to go to Reginald Bay to ask if the Lilys needed help after Locan had been shot. That is, except for Meb, the dressmaker.

Aiby smiled at me as if she could read my mind. I dropped my gaze and blushed, which always happened to me when I was around her. Whenever she was near, I felt cloaked in a state of happy, awkward embarrassment that I didn't know how to protect myself from. I shoved my hands into the pockets of my grandfather's jacket.

The sun had finally set. Reverend Prospero boomed, "Let us begin."

The men responsible for the fire began turning the drill in the hole. Soon, sizzling splinters spread into the air. The first scorching sparks set fire to the bunches of dried heather on the pile. Reverend Prospero watched in silence, his grim face following the sparks as they danced upon the air.

I was wiggling my fingers in my pockets, unable to stay still, when I felt something in the lining of my jacket. I fingered the strange object and tried to free it by moving it slowly so that no one would notice. It was

flat, round, and small like a coin. Inch by inch I managed to push it out of a hole in the pocket that it must have originally gotten in through.

I examined it in the glare of the fire. It really was a coin. An ancient one. How long had my grandfather owned this jacket? I flipped the coin between my fingers. There was a head on each side of the coin: a man's face on one side, a woman's face on the other.

"Uh-oh," I whispered. There was one thing that my father had warned me about this evening: make absolutely sure not to have even the smallest metal object with us. Not a key nor a coin — nothing at all. He'd told me it was extremely important. Another one of those traditions steeped in mystery, I guess. And so I'd put all my keys into my secret box beneath my bed where I keep all my precious things.

I bit my lip, worried without knowing why. One of the branches of dried heather caught fire, so McStay lifted it above his head in order to slip it underneath the bonfire. Pretending to cough from the smoke, I used the distraction to take one, two, three quick steps back, leaving the circle of men. I turned abruptly and threw the strange coin toward the sea with all my strength. I didn't hear it fall due to the flames crackling behind me.

A yellow flame had spread among the dry branches.

It rose rapidly, like a cloak of light. I rejoined the circle, inching closer until the flames tickled my cheeks.

Then Mr. Everett pointed at the horizon and said, "Look." Bonfires had been lit on several of the other islands in the bay. Counting ours, there were seven in all.

Inspired by a vague sense of unity, we stood tall and silent, relishing the warmth of the crackling fire. Then, after the flames had died down and the stacked-up pieces of wood had collapsed inward, all the men in the circle picked up a stone from the ground. One by one, the men placed the stones around the embers.

My father handed stones to me and my brother. "Put them in front of your feet at the edge of the fire and memorize the point of the circle where you are now."

My stone was yellow and as sharp as a knife. I arranged it next to Doug's and heard them click against each other. Aiby placed two stones since Mr. Lily couldn't bend over to do it himself.

Then we walked in a line, one by one, back toward the village. Only Reverend Prospero remained at the top of the hill. He made the sign of the cross in front of himself. Then, once he was fairly sure no one could see him, he made another gesture toward the sea: he intertwined his fingers over his heart, then stretched out his left hand as if he were greeting the night.

Chapter THREE

DELAYS, WATCHES, & WAITING

Our little group set off slowly along the same path we'd come. We were headed to the Greenlock, the only pub in Applecross.

As we walked along in single file, I tried to slip away from my dad so I could stroll alongside Aiby and her father. I kept walking slower, carefully retreating step by step toward the end of the line where they were. When I reached Mr. Everett and Seamus, I walked in stride with them a bit in order to listen to what they were saying about the starry sky. It seemed especially bright to me that night.

Mr. Everett was a retired university professor who had withdrawn from the bustle of the city. He was a

friendly person who spent most of his time smoking a pipe and chatting amiably. I didn't think his Curious Traveler shop made much money, but that didn't seem to bother him.

"Do you know how to read the stars, Everett?" Seamus asked.

"No, but I'd certainly like to learn," Mr. Everett said.

"I don't know how to, either," Seamus said. "I doubt I could even read their instruction manual."

"My mother knew how to read palms," Mr. Everett said. "And she said that being able to read the lines in the palm was just like being able to read the stars."

Seamus nodded solemnly. "They're the imprints of time," he said.

Mr. Everett smiled. "The handwriting of time," he said. He noticed me at that point and sought my approval with a nod.

But I looked away and I drew back sharply, practically landing in Aiby's arms. "It's important to learn how to read signs, don't you agree?" she teased me. She knew how hard it was for me to learn any language, let alone enchanted ones.

"I suppose," I admitted, more amused than embarrassed. I quickly changed the subject. "I didn't expect to see you at the funeral."

"Dad insisted," Aiby said.

"Why?" I asked.

Aiby shrugged. "Because he did." Then she took me by the arm. "But tomorrow we need to speak to you and Meb," she whispered, clinging to me. "We have some very bad news."

"What kind of bad news?" I asked.

"It's not the kind of thing you can talk about at a funeral," Aiby said. "But I've never seen Dad this worried before."

I grunted. "Terrific," I said. "What kind of danger are we going face this time around? Stone giants? Green Men who gamble for souls? Werewolf Sheep?"

"I said we'd talk about it tomorrow. At the store," she said in a conspiratorial tone.

I noticed Reverend Prospero was bringing up the rear along with two fishermen.

"I have to be at the church tomorrow morning at eight," I reminded her. "For work."

"Meb is coming by at nine," Aiby said. "Try to be there if you can, Finley."

"I don't know if I can, Aiby," I said.

"Then come before going to see Prospero," she added. "At six."

The mere idea of pedaling along the coastal road at

six in the morning made me gag. I felt a shiver in my bones — the kind you get when you put your feet onto the cold floor an hour before dawn.

I pointed to the brightly lit pub shining warmly at the end of the path. "Can't we talk about it at the Greenlock?" I asked.

Aiby shook her head. "We can't stay. We have the Good Night Heels to take us back home, but unfortunately they're only safe to use before midnight."

"I could go with you," I offered.

Aiby released my arm and smiled at me. "That's nice of you, but it's not necessary. But if you really want to do something for me . . ."

I would've jumped off a cliff for her, but it didn't seem necessary to tell her that. At this point, I had to admit to myself that I'd fallen in love with her. The thought had been bothering me for days now. I felt like a guy in one of those romance novels. You see, mine was an impossible love. Not only was Aiby six inches taller than me, but I also suspected she was two years older and liked my brother, Doug. Three simple clues that made me realize I was out of the running before the race had even begun. My brother was captain of the rugby team and had already explained to me several times that this impresses girls right away.

" . . . jump off a cliff?" I half-muttered in response. My thoughts were too jumbled to get them back in order.

Aiby laughed and pulled an antique silver timepiece out of her pocket, complete with a chain. "Nothing as dramatic as that," she said. "I just want you to always keep this with you."

I may have been naive, but I wasn't completely foolish. Aiby and her father's store was filled with magical objects, so I was pretty certain that this seemingly worn-out watch had some sort of mysterious power.

"What is it?" I asked, narrowing my eyes.

"It was my mother's watch," Aiby said. She wound its spring, checked that its only hand was lined up to the correct hour, and then placed it in my palm.

"Will you promise that you aren't playing a strange practical joke on me?" I asked. "Like shipping me off to Patagonia or summoning a White Rabbit?"

"You can rest assured, and so can we," Aiby said, nodding at her father. He was leaning on my brother and limping along behind us. "Dad and I were thinking that this Second Chance Watch could give you some extra protection."

"Protection from what?" I asked.

Aiby gently closed my fingers around the watch. "Do you mind if we talk about this tomorrow?"

I grumbled. We walked in silence for several minutes.

When we arrived at the paved part of the coastal road, I blurted out, "You know what I can't stand about all this magic business? The mysterious expressions. Things like, 'You'll know when the time is right. You'll figure it out in the end. We'll talk about it tomorrow.'"

Click-clack. I turned to look at the source of the sound and saw that Aiby was gone. My brother was holding his arm up to support someone who was no longer there. "What happened, Doug?" I asked.

"Man, I have no idea," Doug said. "Mr. Lily thanked me for helping him, clicked his heels together, and poof! They both disappeared."

The Good Night Heels, I realized.

Doug made a face like he smelled sour milk. "The Lilys are so weird."

My brother and I continued toward the pub where the others had gone. He noticed the silver timepiece I was holding. "Where'd you get that?" he asked.

"Aiby gave it to me before she disappeared," I said.

"Looks like it's made of iron," Doug said, one eyebrow raised.

I examined it with my fingers. "Or silver."

"You'd better hide it before Dad sees it," Doug said.

"Otherwise he'll think you brought it to keep away some ghost."

"What ghost?" I asked.

My brother ignored my question and pushed open the door to the Greenlock. The clamor from the people inside hit us like a rolled-up newspaper to the face.

My long-eared dog leapt into my arms. "Patches!" I exclaimed. Dad hadn't let me bring him to the bonfire, so Patches had stayed at the pub with my mom the whole time. His nose was smudged with oats.

"Did you have a good time, boy?" I asked.

Patches whined softly. I checked to see who had gathered at the pub. More or less everyone in Applecross was there, it seemed. Michael had resumed his command post behind the bar. My mother was talking to Mrs. Bigelov from the deli. Mrs. Santangelo was arguing with the Dogberry sisters. In one corner, Meb was joking with a farmer whose name I didn't remember. In the opposite corner, McBlack was sitting as stiffly as death itself.

The tables were loaded with raw prawns, Beltane egg cakes, and bannock (oat bread that Patches had apparently sampled).

Doug had joined Piper the fisherman and Seamus the TV antenna installer. They were talking about the

stones we put around the fire when the blaze had begun to die down.

"I saw my folks do it once. It protects the fire from ghosts," Piper said with a lisp. "To your health!" he added, then raised a pint of beer and drank half of it in a single gulp.

Seamus agreed with him. He polished off his own ale, then added, "The ghosts from the moor will try to steal some of the fire. But with all those stones there, they won't be able to get to it." He shivered.

"So what?" Piper said.

"They'll get angry at one of us," Seamus said.

I looked at Doug for an explanation, but he just shrugged.

Seamus glanced at me. "Tomorrow morning you should go back and see which stone they've moved."

"Why?" I asked.

"Whoever placed that stone will be the first to die," he said grimly. "Like old lady Cumai."

"Well that's twisted," I said.

"But true!" Seamus said. "And that's not all . . ."

Seamus trailed off when a large hand came down on his shoulder. The voice of the Reverend roared in his ears. "Enough of this childishness!" he bellowed. "Hasn't

coming to church every Sunday done you any good, Seamus?"

"Prospero, bringer of storm tidings!" Piper exclaimed. "Let Seamus speak — he's getting to the best part!"

"No, I am not going to let him speak," the Reverend said. "It's almost midnight, gentlemen. And it seems to me that we still have a few matters to discuss." Seamus shrank beneath the Reverend's heavy hand.

Piper gulped down the rest of his beer and promised he'd tell me the story another time. As he moved away, he added, "Assuming there *is* a next time!"

Midnight arrived. Many of the others left in a hurry, giving various excuses. Mr. Everett picked up his oilskin jacket and disappeared. Someone else laughed, talking loudly. I grabbed an oatmeal scone and left. I thought I heard Mr. Everett's footsteps drawing away in the direction of the dock, but I must have been wrong since his house was in the opposite direction.

I watched the dark contours of the islands, wondering who had lit the other fires that evening since the boats were all ashore on the beach. The sea was calm and the starlight reflected peacefully on the water. I heard an outboard motor in the distance and imagined that some fishermen were already going out to sea.

I leaned back against the outer wall of the pub and thought about many different things, most of which involved Aiby. "That girl is going to drive me nuts," I muttered, taking a bite of my scone.

"Psst! Hey!" came a soft voice not more than ten steps away from me. "McPhee! Is that you?"

GOOD *Night* HEELS

ENCHANTED EMPORIUM

APPLECROSS, SCOTLAND

Good kids who don't want to return home late can rely on the Good Night Heels to get them home on time. Whoever wears them can quickly return home by tapping the heels together. However, if used after midnight, the fickle footwear might mete out fearful punishments instead.

Chapter
FOUR

WHISPERS,
WORDS, &
SCREAMS

I looked for the source of the whisper, but I only saw
the shore, the beached boats, and the cars parked in
front of the pub in a fishbone pattern.

"I'm here! In the van!" came the soft voice again.

I passed the rest of my scone to Patches and
approached Barragh McBlack's mud-covered van. The
back of the van was empty except for a little birch sapling
in a pot, held down by two crossed ropes.

"Um, where in here?" I asked, looking around inside.
I was sure that McBlack had already gone home, but
apparently not, since the van was still there.

"I'm the plant!" came a voice from the container.
"Can you hear me?"

I blinked a couple of times. I'd heard, but it didn't

make any sense. I leaned against the van, wondering what had been in that scene.

The plant spoke again. "It's me! Somerled!"

I jumped. Somerled was McBlack's daughter — a mysterious little girl with green skin. I had glimpsed her through the windows of Scary Villa when I'd climbed onto its roof to steal the Sherwood Compass.

"Listen — whoever you are," I muttered, thinking someone was playing a prank on me. "How about you just come out? Where are you hiding? Under the van?"

"I'm in my dad's attic at Scary Villa," it replied.

"Then how am I hearing your voice?" I asked.

"It's called Virdilingua, Finley McPhee," the talking tree explained. "It's the old art of speaking through the branches of trees, like the wind. One of two tricks I still know how to do!"

"And the other trick?" I asked.

"You'll see the other trick tomorrow, Finley!" said the sapling. "I need to talk to you about Cumai. And I have to give you something very important before it's too late!"

"Wow," I said. "It seems like everyone wants to talk to me tonight. It must be my lucky evening."

"I know," the plant said.

I frowned. "And how do you know that?" I asked.

"Meet me at the Black Birch in Reginald Bay," the sapling said. "Tomorrow at ten — on the dot!"

It was a more manageable appointment than the morning meeting Aiby had suggested, but the fact remained that I had to be at Prospero's at eight for work.

I tried to reason with the sapling, but all I got in response was the dry rustling of branches and the command: "Tomorrow at ten, at the Black Birch!"

"Wait!" I repeated. "Is it really you, Somerled? Did you really appear in the woods a hundred years ago?"

"I strongly doubt that, kid," interrupted the voice of the district policeman Bobby Thorne. He had just exited the pub and was getting ready to drive home in his car. He looked at the birch in the container in McBlack's van, then at me. He snorted loudly. "I'm not what you'd call an expert, kid, but it seems unlikely that this sapling starting growing a century ago. It's probably two years old, at the most."

We stood there in silence for a moment.

"I'd better go home," Bobby Thorne concluded, turning on his car lights. "And maybe you'd better go home, too."

The plastic seat cover crackled under his weight as he climbed in. Bobby Thorne grasped the steering wheel as if it were a life jacket. "The cakes were really great,"

he said, looking straight ahead at no one in particular. "Really great. And the beer, too." Then he drove off.

What a weird night, I thought.

A half hour later, we headed home. Dad drove. Patches slept, curled up between my feet. Mom remarked that old lady Cumai would have been glad to know that almost everyone had come to her funeral and that it had been a lovely idea to arrange the little afterparty. She claimed there was no reason to be so sad at funerals. I didn't bother to argue.

I could tell that Dad wasn't sad, though he was serious and worried. He kept looking at the sea as if he were waiting for something terrible to happen.

By time we parked in the front yard at the farm, it was one in the morning. I let Patches climb out. All of us headed straight for the house.

"Too bad your friend Aiby didn't stay," Doug said as we opened the door.

"Yeah," I said.

"I agreed to drop by and see her tomorrow," Doug said.

"Oh, really? What time are you going?" I asked.

The door to the house closed behind us. Mom and Dad had stayed back in the front yard to talk.

"At 11:00 or 11:30," Doug said. He took off his shoes

and sighed. "Maybe I can persuade her to go on a picnic in the boat afterward."

Patches sniffed the air. The fur rose on his back and he bared his teeth. I bent down. "What's going on, Patches? What is it?"

Patches growled toward the stairs that led to the bedrooms. "Is someone up there?" I whispered.

Doug didn't hesitate. He grabbed a poker from the fireplace and went up the stairs two at a time, Patches a few steps behind him. I did my best to act manly by picking up a broom and following him cautiously like a spy in the movies. Once we were upstairs, we quickly checked the hallway in both directions. The door to the bathroom was ajar but no one was inside.

Patches growled louder and began to scratch at the door to my room.

"He's in there," I said softly.

Doug raised the poker. We drew closer and heard a strange noise come from behind the door. A sort of swishing sound followed by a rolling noise.

I thought about what I'd hidden in the box under my bed. *My collection!* I thought.

I heard my parents' voices in the yard. "Doug," I whispered, "Maybe we should get Dad."

In response, my brother slammed his shoulder into

the door and burst inside. Patches followed, barking furiously. I raised my broom and yelled, "Attack!" or something equally stupid.

Something leapt at me and I raised my arms to protect myself. I heard the crash of falling objects. In the dim light from the hallway, I saw a raven slamming against the glass of the half-open window.

"Get out of here, you ugly beast! Go away!" Doug shouted, shaking the poker at it. Stunned, the raven flapped its wings, slipped through the window, and flew away. Doug stuck his head outside to make sure it was really gone. He jerked his head back inside and said, "It was just a raven."

"Ravens don't fly at night," I pointed out.

"You're wrong," Doug said.

"No, I'm not," I said.

"You are," he said. "There are even more outside."

I shrugged. Doug rolled his eyes. Slowly, his face took on the look of someone dumbfounded. I followed his gaze and saw that the wall of my room was covered with dark scratches.

"What the devil?" my brother murmured.

I turned on the light. The message on the wall hadn't been written in the common alphabet. It was the Enchanted Language, the forgotten magicians' alphabet.

The letters sparkled. I tried to read them, but they shifted and moved as if alive.

Doug beat me to the punch and read the words aloud. "If you really want to play this game, find . . ." he trailed off. I don't know how he'd managed to learn, but reading it was child's play for him.

"Find what?" I asked.

Doug shrugged. "That's all it says. What 'game,' bro? And who did this?"

I looked around. My fake Stegosaurus bones, lens-shaped rocks, quail feathers, and all the items in my little collection of odd objects lay scattered on the floor. Doug opened the wardrobe and my clothes fell on top of him. Those dirty birds had gone through everything.

"Askell!" I exclaimed, diving under my bed to retrieve the box where I kept my key to the Emporium.

There were feathers everywhere under my bed. My box had been opened. As I retrieved it, my heart skipped a beat. It was empty. I lifted up the false bottom and let out a sigh of relief. The scorpion key was still there. I put it around my neck.

"What's going on, Finley?" Doug asked. "Who the heck is Askell?"

"I'm not actually sure," I answered. "But as soon as I find out, you'll be the first to know."

Chapter
FIVE

THE COOK,
THE SEAMSTRESS, &
THE GIRL

We closed the door to my room before my parents came up, and then pretended everything was fine. Doug helped me clean up the mess and move the wardrobe to cover the writing on the wall.

The mere idea of lying down in my bed made me feel sick to my stomach, so I fell asleep in Doug's room instead. I sank into a sweaty sleep, swallowed up by dreams I couldn't remember later.

When I awoke, it was morning. Doug had already gone to work with my father. I went into the bathroom and stood there for a few moments, looking at my reflection in the mirror. *So what will happen today?* I wondered.

It was already 7:30. I brushed my teeth, got dressed, and went downstairs without even opening the door to my room again.

"Are you going to the Reverend's, Finny?" my mom asked. The blood in my veins froze.

Finny. It was a hideous nickname. Worse than Viper, even.

"Come on, Ma," I groaned. "I'm almost fourteen."

She smirked.

I felt anxious for some reason, so I sat down and waited for my cup of coffee. Ever since I could remember, no matter what time I awoke, my mother was already there to make me breakfast. And I think that was the case for Doug and Dad, too, but I was never up early enough to find out.

"You don't always have to be here to make us breakfast," I said.

She raised an eyebrow. "Oh? Then who should do it?"

I sat down at the table, letting her serve me. "I volunteer Doug."

Mom chuckled. "Maybe," she said.

As if on cue, my brother burst into the house, banging the front door. Then he tripped and nearly fell on his face.

My mother and I laughed. "Maybe not," she said.

Doug eyed us warily but said nothing as he made his way upstairs.

I ate a slice of apple coffeecake, slipped another slice into my backpack, and tossed a third to Patches — making sure Mom didn't notice. Then I headed out back to get my new bicycle, which had been a gift from Lily and Locan to replace the one I'd destroyed shortly before.

I brushed off the invisible seat, slung my regular old backpack on my back, and pushed the bike into the yard.

"Hey, bro!" Doug called as I was leaving. "Don't do anything stupid, all right? And when you get back, you need to tell me what's going on with the ravens, okay?"

"Okay," I said, putting my feet on the pedals.

My brother came down the porch steps and struck a pose like our mom does. "I mean it, Finny," he said.

"Don't call me that!" I said.

He tried to grab my ear, but I dodged him.

"Don't you dare get into trouble again," Doug said. "Seriously, Finley. I'm your brother."

"You finally noticed," I said with a smirk. "I was hoping you would."

Doug smirked back. "Listen, I know there are things we can't talk about with our parents. Things they wouldn't understand . . ."

41

I bit my tongue to stop from saying that he probably wouldn't understand most of what I'd seen, either.

Doug continued. "But I want you to know I'm here. Whatever you're going to chase after, I'm here. You can count on me."

Wow, I thought. *If I heard this conversation on TV, I'd change the channel to avoid getting cavities.* But to be honest, I kind of liked hearing it from my brother.

I nodded. "Don't tell anyone anything," I said.

"About what?" Doug asked.

"Anything," I repeated.

Doug gave me a thumbs-up. I waved goodbye, ignoring the weird lump in my throat.

I began pedaling. I didn't know it yet, but the longest day of my life was just beginning.

The air along Baelanch Ba, the coastal road, was crisp, clear, and dusted with salt. I pedaled to Reverend Prospero's rectory at top speed. Patches trotted at my side, his tongue hanging out.

To my surprise, the rectory was closed and the Reverend was gone. Only the choirmaster, Mr. McStay, and Miss Finla (his housekeeper) were there. After the death of old lady Cumai, Miss Finla was officially the oldest person in the village.

42

"No, we don't know how long the Reverend will be away," the choirmaster said to me, stroking his long, sinister beard. I could never remember his real name.

"And he didn't say anything about me?" I asked. "We'd agreed to meet at eight to start my new job." I checked my watch. "And it's almost eight."

The choirmaster glanced at McStay, who then glanced at the housekeeper. Miss Finla quickly shuffled back into the rectory.

I listened to the sounds coming from inside, which made me realize Miss Finla was moving things around. I realized she was looking for a note. "Can I consider myself free from my commitment?" I said before she could turn up a list of chores left by the Reverend.

"I'd say so," the choirmaster replied.

I walked past the front windows of the Curious Traveler, Mr. Everett's souvenir shop. It turned out to be closed, too. I saw Meb just as she was leaving her shop.

"Hi, Finley!" she said.

"Meb, do you know where the Reverend is?" I asked.

"Nope," Meb said. She turned the sign on her tiny store from *OPEN* to *CLOSED* and offered me a ride in her car. I declined since I had my bike, but saw an impressive leather suitcase on the passenger seat of her car.

"What's that?" I asked, pointing.

Meb shrugged her shoulders. "Oh, that? It's a special suitcase that wasn't staying shut. I think I've managed to fix it. Now it should only activate when it's outside the house, and only when it's commanded to depart."

I nodded despite my complete confusion. Our tasks for the Enchanted Emporium were very different. I'd received the scorpion key and was its defender. Meb had the bee key, which made her the shop's repairperson.

Meb caught me eyeing the suitcase with a raised eyebrow. She handed me a pair of glasses with polished brass frames. "Try these on," she said.

"How do they work?" I asked.

"You put them on your face, silly," she said.

I shrugged and put on the glasses. I looked at Patches, then at Meb.

"Nothing's happening," I said.

"Perfect!" Meb exclaimed with a big smile. She tied her hair behind her head with a yellow elastic band. "According to the *Big Book of Magical Objects*, these are phobo-sensitive glasses." Meb raised her hand to stop me from speaking. "Yes, you heard that correctly! Not *photo*sensitive — *phobo*-sensitive. They can see fear."

"You fixed them, then?" I asked.

"It took me three days to figure out how they worked," Meb said. "I studied them, took them apart, then put them back together. Maybe one day I'll show you how to work with magical objects."

"I'd rather not," I said. I had no intention of getting chased by a bloodthirsty sword or anything remotely similar to that experience ever again.

Meb shrugged. "At first, I was absolutely sure that Locan — I mean, Mr. Lily — had just given me a pair of regular old glasses. That is, until I put them on yesterday evening to watch a movie. And suddenly, in the middle of a scene, the lenses turned completely black. Then they went back to normal at the end of the scene. That's when I figured it out!"

"Figured what out?" I asked.

"That the phobo-sensitive lenses get dark a moment before something scary happens. That way you won't see anything that might frighten you."

"Brilliant!" I said, and I meant it.

"Best used for watching horror movies, I'd say," Meb answered, taking back the glasses. "What do you say? Shall we go? You sure you don't want a ride?"

Patches barked. "I know, Patches. You'd rather go with her," I said. "But a little run will do you good,

don't you think?" I waved goodbye to Meb and started pedaling.

The Enchanted Emporium was just north of town in Reginald Bay. An unusual, arrow-shaped sign pointed toward the store, though it changed direction depending on where you were standing when you looked at it. To get to the Emporium, you had to cross the old, incinerated oak forest. Then you had to follow the white, oval stones that bordered Reginald Bay. The area had been named in honor of the Lily family's ancestor whose red-hulled ship had gotten wrecked there. Aiby had explained to me that the Enchanted Emporium — which was sheltered by the cliff in a spot protected from the wind — had been built from the red boat's wood.

The seagulls guarding the store twirled over the roof in ever-widening circles. Meb's little car had already arrived. I pedaled hard and covered the last stretch at top speed, Patches barking furiously at the seagulls as he ran.

Meb and Mr. Lily were sitting in front of the shop. Meb was in a wicker rocking chair rocking slowly. Mr. Lily was perched on a cushion that floated in the air inside what looked like a big soap bubble. The bubble was suspended between the wide-open mouths of two opalescent snakes. Inside the bubble, a golden powder swirled. Locan Lily was wearing an ivory tunic. His eyes were closed and his face was lined with deep wrinkles. His pale hair, which was usually wild, fell limply to his shoulders.

I approached cautiously. Patches didn't follow. Instead, he stretched out on the ground next to the bike and placed his nose between his paws to survey us from a safe distance.

"Tell your dog that our family won't harm him," Mr. Lily mumbled from inside his bubble.

I hesitated. Was he actually encouraging me to talk to my dog?

"Each family has animal guardians," Meb said, reading the confusion on my face. "You have Patches. The Lilys have the seagulls."

"And Askell has the ravens!" I recalled. I quickly recounted to them what had happened in my room the night before.

"He wanted to frighten you," Mr. Lily said, his eyes still closed.

"Mission accomplished," I admitted. "He even scared Doug a little."

"Doug's not a problem," Aiby said from inside the Enchanted Emporium.

"I know," I confirmed. "I made him swear not to talk about it with anyone."

"Of all the magical animals," Mr. Lily said, "ravens are to be feared the most. Though very few of them are also Borderpassers."

"Of course, of course," I muttered sarcastically. For just one day I wished the Lily family would stop assuming that I always knew what they were talking about. "In fact, Patches is a champion Borderpasser — especially if you throw a tennis ball into another dimension."

Aiby laughed. "Goofball" she said, joining us outside. "A Borderpasser is someone who can pass from our world to the world of magic. It's a very rare and important ability." And as if to help me better understand the concept, she came over to me and gave me a kiss on the cheek.

I certainly felt myself transport from my world to the world of magic. I stood there, looking at her. She was wearing a pair of torn jeans and a checkered shirt tied just above her belly button. She handed Meb a cup of steaming tea and brought another toward the bubble that her father was floating in.

Mr. Lily stretched out a hand, grabbed the cup, and pulled it inside the sphere. Miniscule sparkles of confetti-like light scattered across the surface.

"Dad's getting healed by a Naga Bubble of Silence," Aiby explained, since neither Meb nor I could stop staring at her floating father. "It is said to have been created in the Patala, the Naga's subterranean kingdom." I raised an eyebrow at her. "The Naga are snake-like people," she added.

I pointed to the swirling, golden powder. "What's that inside it?" I asked.

"It takes away pain, heals bodily wounds, and relaxes the mind," Aiby said. "Anyway, weren't we talking about Askell's ravens and Borderpassers?"

I nodded.

"Want a cup of tea while we chat?" she asked.

I decided then and there that I'd never be able to keep up with the Lilys. "Why not," I said.

Naga Bubble of Silence

The Naga Bubble of Silence is one of the ancient meditational objects from Patala, the subterranean realm of Indian deities. If you rest within this bubble and meditate, the influence of the Naga serpents will heal you. In fact, its aura can cure any non-fatal wound as long as the user concentrates hard enough and spends sufficient time inside the bubble.

ENCHANTED EMPORIUM

Chapter
SIX

FAMILIES,
HOUSES, &
OTHER WORLDS

"The families are very worried," Mr. Lily said while Aiby grabbed my tea. "Even we Lilys don't feel safe. That's why we called you both here."

"Thanks," I said to Aiby, taking the tea. It smelled of strange spice and burned my tongue upon sipping it. I sat down on the floor with my legs crossed and waited to hear the rest of the story.

"Aiby and I wrote to the other families to ask for a meeting with all the representatives," Mr. Lily said. "It's something I should have done on the day the store opened, when we first noticed that something was happening. I just didn't think it would get to this point."

Mr. Lily slowly sipped his tea, his eyes still closed.

"In order to understand what I'm about to tell you, first you need to know a few things," he said. "The Enchanted Emporium is over a thousand years old now. Ever since our ancestor Diamond Lily began writing the first pages of the *Big Book of Magical Objects* and opened the first Emporium in China, seven families have continued to take turns passing on the four keys that we now hold. This has happened without interruption, generation after generation after generation, following the code of rules that Diamond Lily decided on with the other families. Their pact has remained intact to this day for exactly one reason: it was a fair pact. Fair to us, the People of Time, who live in this part of the world, and fair to the Others, the magical creatures who live in that part of the world where time cannot reach. We shopkeepers call it the Hollow World."

Mr. Lily opened his eyes. His pupils were the color of gold. "The Hollow World has a thousand other names. The Scottish call it *sith*, the Irish call it *sidhe*, the Welsh refer to it as *cwni*, and the Portuguese identify it as *moura encantada*. But none of them describe it well."

I let out a sigh. Just like in class, it was noticed right away. "Is something unclear, Finley?" Mr. Lily asked.

"I get most of it," I said. "It's just this last part about the Hollow World that confuses me."

"What about it?" Mr. Lily asked.

"I don't exactly know how to say this, Mr. Lily, but it would be pretty hard to get a science teacher to believe any of this, don't you think? I mean, what is this Hollow World? A world inside our world?"

"No one can say exactly which of the two worlds contains the other," Mr. Lily said.

"I bet we're on the inside track," I said with a smirk, earning a playful kick from Aiby.

Mr. Lily closed his eyes again and continued solemnly. "What we can say with certainty is that there is a world that exists in time, which is the world of the here and now, where things are born, grow, age, and disappear. There also exists a world of magic, where none of that occurs. Or at least, where it doesn't occur according to the same rules as in the world of time."

"Is that why you gave me the watch with only one hand?" I asked Aiby.

"That's a Second Chance Watch, Finley. It's a very powerful artifact," Mr. Lily said. "So powerful that its mechanism only works once in a lifetime."

"In whose lifetime?" I asked.

Mr. Lily continued, ignoring my question. "It was built in the middle of the seventeenth century by a Dutch astronomer who had just lost the love of his life.

From the moment it was brought to the Emporium, it's been one of the family's most guarded treasures. That is, until Aiby insisted we give it to you."

I glanced at Aiby, surprised the decision had been hers. But she was watching her father.

"Always keep it wound, Finley," Mr. Lily said. "If something irreparable should happen, you can try to move the single hand of the watch to get a second chance."

"Do you mean I can go back in time?" I asked.

Mr. Lily nodded. "You can go back in time a little bit, with everything on your person, yes. But the *Big Book of Magical Objects* says you can only do that once in your lifetime. That's how second chances work. Should there come a time when life provides you with one, do not waste the opportunity, for it will never come again."

"Did he succeed?" I asked. "I mean, did the astronomer who built the watch get his second chance?"

"Actually, no," Mr. Lily replied. "Christian Huygens discovered Titan, a moon of Saturn, and hypothesized that there might be life on the other planets in the solar system . . . but he never did find the woman he was hopelessly in love with ever again."

"Then it doesn't work so well," I muttered, fingering the Second Chance Watch in my pocket."

"It only works if you believe it will," Mr. Lily said.

"I have my doubts," I admitted.

"That's exactly it," Mr. Lily said. "If you have any doubts, no magic will work. That's the Great Rule."

"Okay, Mr. Lily," I said. "But I still don't understand."

"Understanding is the first of the Great Illusions of Time," he replied. "It's not at all necessary to understand something in order for it to work."

"I'm in perfect agreement with you about that," I said. "But you'll never convince the Widow Rozencratz."

"And who is this Rozencratz?" Mr. Lily asked.

"She's the superintendent at my school," I said. "She's making me repeat a grade because I did too many things without understanding why I did them."

"That's often the case with things that aren't real," Mr. Lily said.

"School isn't real?" I asked.

"Exactly. Many things don't really exist here," Mr. Lily said. "The things that really do exist aren't the things that are here."

"I'd like to see you try to convince Miss Rozencratz of all this," I said.

"You still don't understand?" Mr. Lily asked, but it didn't seem like a question.

I shrugged.

"I didn't tell you the things that don't exist do not exist at all," Mr. Lily droned. "I only meant that they don't exist *here*."

I cradled my head between my hands. "It's all just too complex, Mr. Lily," I said. "Give me a sword and I'll fight for your store without a moment's hesitation. But please don't expect me to understand what the heck you're talking about."

Mr. Lily narrowed his eyes at me. "Do you doubt whether magic exists?"

"Of course not, Mr. Lily," I said. "I'm not that dumb. I've seen some of the bizarre objects inside the store. I mean, we fought with magical weapons against a giant. We climbed the mountains of Shangri-La."

"Where do you think the giants live?" he asked.

"At the bottom of the sea, I hope," I said.

"And the other creatures you've encountered?" Mr. Lily asked. "The Green Man who played you in a game of cards for ownership of your soul?"

I shook my head. "I don't know, Mr. Lily. They live somewhere else, I know that much. Maybe it's a well hidden place underground, or something. But I don't believe they live in a Hollow World or whatever."

"Why don't you believe in the Hollow World?" he asked.

56

I was starting to get annoyed. "Because I've never seen it, for one thing. Like you said, it's okay not to understand the 'whys' and 'hows' of a thing in order for it to work. But I *do* have to be able to see it to be able to believe in it."

"So you only believe what you see?" Mr. Lily asked.

I thought for a moment. "Yes," I said.

"Then tell me this," Mr. Lily said, leaning forward. "Have you ever seen Greenland?"

"No."

"How about an erupting geyser?"

"No," I said.

"A whale?"

"No, but my brother, Doug —"

"Have you ever seen England?" Mr. Lily interrupted.

"No," I repeated.

"France?"

"No."

"And so you don't believe these countries, animals, or natural phenomena really exist?" Mr. Lily asked.

"Of course they exist!" I blurted out.

"Why?"

"Why? *Why?*" I asked angrily. "Because other people have seen them, obviously."

"Ah!" Mr. Lily exclaimed triumphantly. "So perhaps

you'd like to adjust your original statement and say that you only believe what other people have seen?"

"As long as it's not just one person, then yes," I said.

"Well, luckily for you, it's not just one person who's seen the Hollow World. Dozens, even hundreds have seen it. And they've described it in different ways because they've visited different parts of it. Just as, on the other hand, travelers from the Hollow World would have done when they found themselves in our world, the World of Time. They, too, have described it in different ways, depending on which passage they entered through."

"Passage?" I repeated.

"Openings, portals, passages. Call them whatever you want. The passages are the connections between the two worlds that keep them joined and balance the energy between them. A little bit of magic filters into our world from the Hollow World, and a little bit of faith drifts into the Hollow World from ours."

"Faith?" Meb repeated.

"Their magic seeps through the passages," Mr. Lily explained. "It can accomplish small wonders and alter what normally happens to us every day. It's the magic that the Makers put in magical objects. Faith, on the other hand, consists of the thoughts of people who believe in luck, in miracles — anything they haven't

seen with their own eyes." Mr. Lily paused and looked me square in the eyes. "It percolates into the Hollow World and allows magical creatures to continue to exist. It's always been like this, in perfect equilibrium, so that everything is balanced. And *fair*."

"Just like how the pact between the Enchanted Emporium's families hasn't changed up to now," Meb added.

"Exactly," Mr. Lily said. "Now that the meeting has been called, we'll know in a few days whose home it will be held at. It might be here in Applecross, the Van de Mayas' home in the Netherlands, the Scarsellis' in Argentina, the Legbas' in Mali, the Tiagos' in China, or the Moogleys' place in New Jersey."

I had heard these names before, but never listed one after the other like some sort of spell. I counted them in my head. "One family's missing," I said. "The Askells."

"Oh, they're not missing," Aiby said, getting to her feet. "It's just that we don't think the meeting will happen at their place in Antarctica because it's Semueld Askell's behavior that we need to talk about with the other families."

"Even though Semueld Askell is certainly not our most serious problem," Mr. Lily added.

SECOND CHANCE WATCH

The Second Chance Watch can be used only once and then must be passed on. It can rewind time up to its operating limit of twenty-four hours. Built in the middle of the seventeenth century by the Dutch astronomer Christian Huygens, it failed to help him find someone he had loved and lost. Great caution must be taken with this magical object since second chances only occur once in a lifetime.

Chapter
SEVEN

THE OTHER,
THE OTHERS, &
OURS

I couldn't imagine what could be more serious than Semueld Askell. The man regularly roamed Applecross wrapped in a Cloak of Mirrors, accompanied by a flock of ravens. He awakened a stone giant in order to destroy the Enchanted Emporium. He conjured the Green Man who had wreaked havoc on Applecross. Then he tried to steal the *Big Book of Magical Objects* from the Enchanted Emporium.

"We have information from highly knowledgeable collectors and magicians," Aiby said after a long silence. "And then we received these letters."

Aiby produced two strange-looking envelopes covered with stamps. I recognized the golden lettering on one of them. "This first one is from the Imaginary

Travelers Club," Aiby said, "a group of people especially interested in places that exist out of time. There's also one from the Mystery Society, a conjurers' organization that recently reopened its headquarters in Paris, France. Both letters report disturbances as well as some hard-to-confirm, ugly rumors. Our clients, as you know, are quite eccentric, so their statements aren't always reliable. But the situation is getting difficult now that the Others seem to be angry with us."

Aiby showed us some pages written in elegant script that was full of flourishes.

"Angry? With the four of us?" I asked.

"Not with the four of us in particular, but with the village of Applecross, apparently," Aiby said.

"But why?" I asked.

Mr. Lily sighed. "Because of old lady Cumai's death. She was one of them. One of the Others."

Meb's eyes widened. "She was a magical being?"

"Exactly, Mr. Lily said. "Her death made the others suspicious of us. And now they've sworn to avenge her death."

"Somerled talked to me about Cumai, too," I said. "And she seemed really worried."

They looked at me like I was crazy, so I rushed to explain. "I saw Somerled late yesterday evening at the

pub, after you all left. Actually, I didn't really see her since she wasn't actually there . . . but I *heard* her talking through a plant I found in the back of her father's van." Meb stared at me with a blank look on her face. "I swear it's true! I didn't even believe it at first, but Somerled explained that it was one of the two tricks she still could do. She called it something like verde . . . verdelenza . . ."

"Virdilingua," Aiby said.

"That's it! And she asked me to meet her this morning at ten," I said. Since Meb, Aiby, and Locan Lily kept staring at me in apparent confusion, I added, "Don't you know who I'm talking about? Somerled McBlack? She has green skin? Lives in Scary Villa? I think she's a magical being, too. So if these people are really angry with us, then maybe she can help us!"

More silence followed. I pulled the Second Hand Watch out from my pocket and checked the time. "I'm supposed to meet her like right now," I said.

"Where?" asked Aiby.

"To tell you the truth, I'm not quite sure," I said. "I wanted to ask you about that, but then Mr. Lily started telling the whole story of the Hollow World and I forgot all about it."

Aiby touched my shoulder. "Did she at least say the name of a place?" she asked.

"She just said we'd meet at ten in the morning at the Black Birch in Reginald Bay and that's why I thought you might know where that is," I said in a single breath.

Aiby glanced at her father. "I know where that is."

"Great!" I said. "Where?"

"The Black Birch is the tree that first caught fire and burned down the rest of Applecross forest," Mr. Lily said.

"Oh," I said. "That doesn't sound like a great place to meet."

"It sure doesn't," Meb agreed.

"However, it is what it is and is not something else," Mr. Lily said. "So hurry up and go!"

Aiby disappeared into the store. As soon as I'd reached my bike, Patches suspected we were about to do something exciting and started wagging his tail.

Aiby came back as I was already pushing my bike up the path and suggested I leave it where it was. She shoved a handful of objects into my backpack and said, "The shortest path is to climb up that way."

I looked in the direction she was pointing and nearly fainted. There was a hundred-foot ascent via huge, white, egg-shaped boulders stacked atop one another.

"That looks unsafe," I said without slowing my pace.

"True. Put these on," she said, tossing me two

metal plates with strange designs etched into them. She showed me how to attach them to the soles of my shoes.

I did so without uttering a word. Then I followed her up the stones as she climbed. "So," I said, following her. "What are these things?"

"Ossendowski Step Guards," she said.

"Oh, that explains everything, then," I said, hopping from one stone to the next.

Patches was trying to follow us, but he was only able to climb onto the first white stone. He watched me worriedly from his precariously balanced spot. A pair of seagulls circled above him and squawked as if they were mocking him.

"They're Danger Dodgers for Small Explorers," Aiby explained. "They are used to avoid hazards and accidents by making sure you put your feet down in the right places."

"Hmph," I said. "How do they work?"

"You just don't think about anything and walk. Let your instincts guide you, and you should be safe."

Don't think about anything and walk, I thought.

I laughed. "Kind of like what your father said: you just have to believe!"

"Hurry up already," Aiby said. "It's almost ten!"

Chapter
EIGHT

THE CLIFF,
THE BURNT FOREST, &
A LITTLE GIRL

We clambered up from one stone to the next along the path without slipping or sliding even once. The foot thingies Aiby gave me were fantastic. If everything went perfectly, at 11:30 I would still be on a mission to who-knows-where in the forest and Doug wouldn't be able to take Aiby on a romantic boat picnic.

The Ossendowski Step Guards seemed to help me choose the right path, but they didn't make hiking any easier. "By the way, Aiby!" I yelled, stopping to catch my breath.

"What is it now?" she asked.

I wanted to ask how old she was, but the question got stuck in my throat like a bullet in a gun that misfired.

Aiby saw me hesitate. "Is everything okay, Finley?"

I replaced the question I'd had in my mind with a new one. "About these Others . . . if they're really angry with us, what are they capable of doing?"

Aiby shrugged her shoulders. "Oh, I don't know," she said. "They could destroy our world, for instance, or just use this event as an excuse for starting another Magical Revolution so they can destroy the fabric of Time once and for all."

"So, the usual," I joked, starting to jump from stone to stone again. For some reason nothing seemed particularly worrisome as I leapt along. "I was afraid it would be something bad."

I slipped sideways unexpectedly. Aiby caught me just in time.

"Yikes!" I shouted, getting back on my feet. I dusted off my hands and pretended everything was fine even though my knee was throbbing. "Did these Step Guard things break?"

"You were distracted by something," Aiby said, scolding me. "You were thinking, weren't you?"

"That's not true!" I exclaimed. "Well, maybe a little true."

We were facing each other, balanced on one white, egg-shaped rock. Aiby's nose was sprinkled with freckles,

her long hair was frizzy from the wind, and her eyes reflected the slivers of light from the sea.

"I'm just a little worried," I admitted, my voice growing weak.

Aiby nodded, then jumped to a nearby rock. "It is a little worrisome," she said. "Cumai was a Spokesperson, after all."

"A Spokesperson?" I said. I took two jumps behind her. "Like . . . an ambassador for the Others?"

"See?" Aiby said, smiling. "You *can* figure things out on your own!"

"I better stop thinking or I'll slip again," I said. Aiby chuckled.

We reached the tree line of the forest, ending our climb. Aiby ran, continuing to speak. "Usually Spokespersons are very important Others who have chosen to live here."

"They can choose?" I asked.

"Of course they can choose," she said.

We walked over the soft grass, steering clear of the deep hollows in the land that looked like a giant's footprints (which, in fact, is exactly what they were).

"So does that work in reverse, too?" I asked. "I mean, can one of us choose to live among the Others?"

"Yes," said Aiby. "We shopkeepers refer to them as

Migratory Magicians, but they have many different names. Reverend Prospero, for example, would call them saints."

"Reverend Prospero seems to have disappeared," I said. "Maybe he caught a whiff of the danger and left town."

I stopped in the middle of the forest. Beams of light were dancing between the leaves and trunks of the oak trees. Aiby breathed softly and stood still, right in front of me. She was so close that the six-inch height difference between us seemed more intimidating than ever.

We'd reached a small clearing dotted with little blue flowers. The gnarled trunk of a birch tree stood out in the middle of the area. Its dark gray bark looked more like granite split by countless cracks than anything else. It was ancient and in pretty rough shape with only a few shriveled up branches and even fewer leaves. It had grown apart from the other trees in the grove.

As I examined the tree, the shape of a young girl began to appear in the bark. She slipped through a fissure in the trunk as if she were stepping out from behind some drapes. Her legs became visible, then her ankles and feet.

Then, finally, Somerled stood before us, her skin as green as a duck's egg. She had two large green eyes and

long hair the color of motor oil. Her skin was so pale that you could make out her veins and arteries, which seemed more like veins filled with gold than blood. Her fingers were webbed to each other with a thin membrane like those of a frog. Her nails were a lightly flecked pale blue color.

Aiby and I stood there in wide-eyed, stunned silence.

"Sorry I'm late," McBlack's daughter finally whispered. "I couldn't pass through the first time I tried."

I blinked my eyes a couple of times. "You mean pass through . . . the tree?"

Who knows why, but I'd imagined that Somerled would reach us by foot, across the sea, or maybe in a Victorian carriage. Certainly not through the trunk of a birch tree as if it were a bark-covered portal.

"I told you I knew a second trick, Finley McPhee," Somerled said with a smile.

"A trick my dad calls the Core of Kalamos," Aiby whispered. "We had a ring that granted a similar ability."

"My brother and I just called it Tree Passing," Somerled said. She climbed over the roots in her bare feet and stood in front of us. She gave off a slightly sweet but intense scent, like violets. "But that was when we were still . . . in the Other Place."

"In the Hollow World?" I asked.

71

"If that's what you call it," Somerled answered. "And now, if you please, I'd like to properly introduce myself, as it's the polite thing to do." She gracefully turned toward Aiby and curtsied. "Pleased to meet you. My name is Somerled."

"Oh," Aiby said. "I'm Finley's friend."

"You're Aiby Lily, right?" Somerled said. "I've heard so much about you!"

"Really? From who?" Aiby asked.

"From the trees," Somerled said. "They're very happy you've come back to Applecross."

Aiby let out a nervous giggle.

I raised an eyebrow. "Do the trees say anything about me?" I asked, sounding a little insecure.

Somerled gave me a big smile. "They said that I can trust you. That's why I decided to talk to you. Now that we've been face to face, you two certainly seem like a couple of magical spirits."

I blushed. Aiby did, too.

"Well, we're not a couple," I said, watching for Aiby's reaction. "Aiby's a lot older than I am."

"What're you saying?" she said, her eyes like daggers.

"It's true," I said with a smirk.

"No, it's not!" Aiby said.

72

I was getting angry for some reason. "That's not what Doug said," I replied.

"Doug? What does Doug have to do with anything?" Aiby said.

Somerled coughed lightly. "However old you are, Aiby, you'll never be older than I am," she said. "The last time I counted, I was over four hundred years old."

"Over four hundred?" Aiby said. I was thankful for the distraction.

Somerled nodded. "Mr. Ralph Coggeshall wrote a story in a cloth booklet that claimed we were even older than that," she said. "Mr. Keightley, on the other hand, wrote that we were ten years old, at most. He insisted he had been the one to discover us in a forest. The truth is that my brother and I came out of a cave in Suffolk well over four hundred years ago. We weren't able to go back through it. There didn't appear to be anything edible in our new environment, so my brother died. I was luckier than him, I suppose."

Aiby and I remained silent, listening.

"After a long while, I revealed myself to some farmers," Somerled continued. "They spoke to me, but I couldn't understand a single world of what you call 'English.' But they were good people and brought me

to the castle of a knight named Sir Richard of Calne. He had me try every type of food he had. After failing to find anything I could eat, I finally discovered beans. I ate a lot of them and, little by little, recovered my health. Sir Richard kept me hidden in his castle and taught me how to speak. He eventually died, and then his son died, too, while I stayed the same age. I went from house to house, offering gold to anyone who would shelter me. I've figured out how to 'feel' the veins of gold in the earth like how your water diviners sense water underground."

Somerled's voice grew quieter. I could tell that her tale was coming to an end.

"Then, about a dozen years ago," she whispered, "I heard about a man named Barragh McBlack. He didn't have children and had amassed a fortune from his whisky distillery. He was also intending to move here to Applecross, where someone else lived — someone like me, who had come from another world."

"Cumai," I murmured.

"Cumai," Somerled agreed. "And so I decided to pretend to be McBlack's daughter. I moved here with him in hopes of somehow meeting her and speaking to her. Our agreement was that he'd give me room and board in exchange for as much gold as I could find."

Somerled paused, then chuckled. "When he chose to

live at Scary Villa, as they call it in the village, I thought that would be the best solution for me. I didn't want to have too much contact with people during my attempts to return home. Of all the people I spoke to, only three left me with favorable memories of our long discussions. One was a nice Dane named Ludwig Holberg who wanted to write a play about my home world. The second was a distinguished Frenchman, Mr. Verne, who asked me many detailed questions. He used my answers to write a magnificent adventure book, in fact. The third person was old lady Cumai herself, who I came to talk to you about."

I heard grass being trampled, followed by furious howling. I recognized the shaggy shape of my devoted friend as he bounded toward me, energetic as ever.

"Patches!" I cried out. He must have covered the stretch of rocks at a gallop, following his nose. "Good dog, good dog." I rubbed him behind the ears the way he liked.

Patches wasn't convinced that Somerled was safe, but after a bit of scratching, his barking turned to soft whines. Bit by bit he stretched out between the little green girl and me, silent and happy.

STEP GUARDS

№ 96208

Ossendowski designed the Step Guards for his expedition to the Orient. It is said that this particular magical object saved the writer from the countless dangers in which he placed himself. When applied to the soles of one's shoes, the Step Guards guarantee safe passage by shielding the wearer from missteps — but also from discoveries and feelings — as long as one doesn't think too much.

Chapter
NINE

THIEVES,
SHIPWRECKS, &
MURDERERS

Somerled took a deep breath. A gentle breeze shook the oak's branches, making it seem like the whole world was creaking. As we sat in the cool, damp grass, the black birch tree swayed back and forth in the scant light.

"Cumai was murdered," Somerled said, her voice barely above a whisper. "And I know who did it." Before we could ask a single question, she added, "It was a *kinkishin*. A Sidhe soldier."

"My father said Cumai died from a heart attack," Aiby said.

"A 'heart attack' is what it's called in this world," Somerled murmured. "But we call it a Sidhe Strike. The person who inflicts it is called a kinkishin."

"Why are you telling us this?" Aiby asked.

Somerled reached out like a willow and grabbed her toes. "Probably because you're the only people in Applecross who would believe me — other than perhaps Reverend Prospero. But unlike you, he hates fairies and magic except for what's in the book he preaches from. So that left me without much of a choice, don't you agree?"

"Agreed," I said. "So, who killed Cumai?"

"A man with clothing that jingles," Somerled said.

I threw Aiby a concerned glance. Would we need to deal with some sort of armed crusader?

"I didn't see him, but I heard him," Somerled continued. "When the man went to visit Cumai, I was talking to her through the large apple tree in the middle of the mill. The man knocked and she opened the door."

"And then what?" I asked, breathless.

"I couldn't hear anything for several minutes. But when they came closer to the apple tree again, I heard Cumai and that man fighting about something called the Ark of the Passages."

"Did they say exactly that?" Aiby asked, suddenly alarmed. "The Ark of the Passages?"

"Yes. The man was furious. He said he'd sifted through the whole village and that he knew the Ark of the Passages could be hidden in one of only two places: Cumai's house or the Enchanted Emporium."

"How did Cumai respond?" Aiby asked.

"She said that he was crazy. Completely crazy. Then he got even angrier and said, 'You're nothing but an old witch, and you want me to believe you don't know anything about the Ark of the Passages?'"

"Did she know about the Ark?" Aiby asked.

"She said she knew about it perfectly well. That they all knew about it, but not because it was hidden in her house," Somerled said, her voice was trembling.

"Then what happened?" I asked.

"I heard a chair break," Somerled said.

"Were they fighting?" I asked.

"I think so. They kept arguing. The man insisted that this Ark had to be in Applecross, but Cumai kept insisting that it was only a legend. He told her that the most powerful object that had ever been created couldn't be just a legend. Then he shouted, 'You've already talked to Locan Lily about it, right? Where are you two hiding the Ark of the Passages?!'"

Somerled and I saw Aiby's face grow as pale as the leaves before summertime.

"Aiby," I asked. "Do you know what they were talking about?"

"Maybe," she said. Then she added, "Actually, yes. Definitely yes, but I didn't think . . ."

Aiby trailed off. I didn't press her to continue. She didn't say anything else for a while.

"They say it was my great-great-grandfather — Reginald Lily," she said, breaking the silence. "That he had it. And that's why the Others caused his shipwreck along the coast."

"Your grandfather had this Ark of the Passages thing?" I asked.

Aiby shook her head. "It's not true. He never had it. My mother looked for it for a long time, all the way until the day before . . . the day before she died. It had become her obsession. My father's as well. They spent years searching for it across half the world — wherever Reginald Lily had left any traces behind. But they never found it. It doesn't exist. The Ark of the Passages has never existed."

"That man seemed certain of its existence when he murdered Cumai," Somerled whispered. "He was convinced it was hidden somewhere in town. At Cumai's house, or —"

"So how did it end?" I interrupted.

"The last thing I heard Cumai say was, 'Semueld, you're making the biggest mistake of your life. May the Others protect you and may the Dreamer Kings never learn of your stupidity.'"

Semueld, my mind repeated.

The wind tipped the flower petals back and wafted up the smell of the sea.

"After that, he cursed and left the mill," Somerled finished.

"Semueld Askell killed old lady Cumai," I said, feeling suddenly weak. And for the first time since the Green Man had arrived, I felt a real sense of danger in in my gut.

Somerled was staring at me with her big jade eyes. "Do you know him? Do you know who he is?"

"We both know him well," Aiby answered for me. "Rather, I should say we thought we knew him. Because I never would've believed he would go so far."

"He's not one of the Others, right?" Somerled asked.

Aiby shook her head. "No. Semueld Askell is a member of one of the seven families who run the Enchanted Emporium. He's a shopkeeper, like me. Or at least he should have become one after my family's turn."

"And this so-called Ark of the Passages?" I said. "What is it?"

"I don't know," Aiby said. "No one knows. It's little more than a legend now. The most ancient of objects, dating back to the most ancient of magical times. Before the Magical Revolution, from a time when writing didn't

exist. The Ark of the Passages was the first magical object ever created. They say it was a treasure chest that contained the essence of all magic inside it — the connection between the two worlds. But whatever it was or wasn't, it is my father's opinion that the object no longer exists. Perhaps it has gone missing, or, more likely, it has been destroyed."

"So why does Askell think you have it?" Somerled asked.

"Because he's been touched by the legend of the Ark of Passages," Aiby said. "Actually, he's been smudged by it, spreading rumors like a Typhoid Mary, infecting others to believe we have the magical object at the Enchanted Emporium."

"But you don't have it, right?" I asked.

Aiby seemed to shrink. "You don't believe me?"

It was hard to meet her gaze, but that day in the oak forest, I did it. I stared her in the face instead of glancing at my feet in embarrassment. My heart pumped harder and harder in my chest until I had no choice but to lower my eyes first.

"Regardless, Semueld Askell is still coming to look for it," Somerled said.

"Let him come," Aiby replied. "We have nothing to fear. My father, Meb, Finley, and I are protected by the

keys we possess. But you're right about one thing, Forest Being." She put her hands on the ground and crossed her fingers, intertwining them with the blades of grass. "We have to consider all the other people in Applecross. We have to solve this problem the right way."

"I say we let Bobby Thorne know," I said.

"Who's Bobby Thorne?" Aiby asked.

"The district policeman," I said.

"And what do you expect him to do about any of this?" Aiby asked. "It's a question of magic, Finley. The ones we should inform first are the Others."

I glared at her. "And how are we going to inform them?" I asked.

"Last night we used a bonfire," Aiby said. "And they replied in kind."

My eyes widened. I remembered the other bonfires that lit up on the islands in the bay. "Do you mean those were the Others communicating with us?"

"Cumai has a brother," Somerled said quietly. "He's a Guardian of the Passages."

"A brother?" I said.

"He was probably the first to get angry," Aiby explained.

"So you're telling me that one of the Passages is on an island in the bay where we saw the bonfires lit?" I asked.

"Yes, but we don't know which one," Somerled said.

I was flabbergasted. "You've been looking for the Passage back to your home, so why didn't Cumai tell you about it?"

"It's not that simple," Somerled said. "Revealing a Passage is a betrayal. And that's just not something they do. Cumai did leave some hints, though. Sort of."

"What do you mean?" Aiby asked.

"When the man left the mill, Cumai wasn't dead," Somerled said. "She used the last of her energy to get close enough to the apple tree to tell me to look for her brother . . . and to give him this." Somerled opened a packet of leaves and pulled out a key made of dark wood. "I think this is the key to Cumai's mill. Shortly before she died, she managed to press it into the apple tree to pass it to me."

Somerled handed it to me. "I don't know how to figure out which island Cumai's brother is on," she said. "But I hope you are able find it."

The key was light. I wondered if it was hollow inside.

"There's one last thing you should know," Somerled murmured. "This Semueld Askell has to be a Borderpasser. Only a Borderpasser could enter the apple tree room in Cumai's mill."

"Semueld's not a Borderpasser," Aiby insisted.

"How do you know?" I asked her.

"I met him," she said. "I would have noticed it."

"So you're one?" I asked. "A Borderpasser?"

"Yes," she answered.

"And am I?" I asked.

Aiby hesitated. I looked down at Patches and petted him. "I don't think I'm a Borderpasser, Patches," I said.

"The truth is that I'm not sure," Aiby said. "Sometimes it seems like you are, sometimes it doesn't."

I chuckled. "So you're saying I'm inconsistent?"

"My father said you have a strong Voice of Places and that your spirit is one with the spirit of Applecross, but that you're not a Borderpasser," she said. "But I'm not so sure. I suppose, yes, you are inconsistent. Or undecided."

"What do you think?" I asked Somerled.

"You have a strong Magical Voice, Finley," Somerled said. She slowly got to her feet. "But I don't know if you're a Borderpasser."

"So there's no way to know for sure?" I asked.

She and Aiby exchanged glances. "There is one way to find out," Somerled said.

Aiby bit her lower lip. "Yes, there is one way."

I waited for her to finish the thought, but she didn't. *That means it's dangerous,* I realized.

Chapter
TEN

THE BOAT,
THE REEF, &
THE TOWER

Aiby and I said goodbye to Somerled, assuring her that we'd find Cumai's brother and give him the wooden key to the mill. Then we left for the Emporium.

"Good grief! I forgot about your brother!" Aiby said suddenly. She had a look of irritation on her face that made me quite happy.

"You're really not any older than I am?" I asked her.

She snorted as we raced along the path toward the Enchanted Emporium. "Listen, Finley. I'm younger than you think and much older than you hope."

"What's that? A riddle?" I asked.

"It should be enough for you," Aiby said. "Okay?"

"Are you two years older than me?" I asked.

"Finley . . ." she said.

"Are you one year older than me?" I asked.

"FINLEY!" she growled.

"Six months?" I asked in my smallest voice.

Aiby stopped and placed her hands on her hips. "I do not intend to continue this discussion." She started scurrying toward her house.

I waited back for a moment to think. *Six months would be okay,* I thought. *It would match our height difference of six inches. I could handle her being six months older than me.*

I grabbed my dog and tossed him in the air with a surge of hope. In response, I received a surprised yip and grumpy look. For a brief moment I forgot all about the conflict between the two worlds, the mysterious murderers, and the impending danger. All I could think about was how to capture Aiby Lily's heart. I hurried to catch up to her.

As I walked, I realized a lucky coincidence — for those who believe in them, anyway (for the record, I am not one of them). Aiby had just told me that the only way to find out if I was a Borderpasser was to dive from the top of one of the signal towers in Applecross Bay. She'd mentioned a specific one called Sheir Thraid. That tower was several miles south of town. It had a kind of cage

at the top, which the kids in Applecross just called "the gallows." It stuck out of the sea some twenty feet from the shore, marking a low reef along the sea floor that was teeming with crabs.

"Aiby," I said, "I think we should go to Sheir Thraid." I expected her to say no, but asked anyway.

Aiby hesitated for a moment. "Okay," she said, still somewhat agitated by my earlier persistence. "Let's ask Doug to bring us there."

I nodded and smirked. *Doug won't like this one bit,* I thought.

* * *

My brother docked the boat he'd "inherited" from Mr. Dogberry in Reginald Bay. This reminded me that he had recently died of a heart attack. *Could Mr. Dogberry's death have been another Sidhe Strike by Semueld?* I wondered.

Doug barely had enough time to turn off the motor before Aiby asked him to take us for a ride to Sheir Thraid. Doug looked at us as like we were a pair of idiots. He reminded us that only Clever Walter, an ironically named shepherd from Applecross, had ever dived from the tower . . . and he'd split his head open on a rock.

Normally that would've given me pause. But that day in July, things had already taken on a life of their own, and I felt powerless to stop them.

Doug pointed out that it would take several hours to get there and back, so Aiby suggested they have a picnic on the boat. I smiled, hopped on board, and took a seat next to Doug.

"You're kidding, right, Viper?" he whispered to me as Aiby took her place at the bow of the boat. "The picnic was supposed to be just me and her."

"Don't worry, I won't eat anything," I whispered back.

My brother was gripping the rudder like he wanted to snap it in two. "I can't believe you managed to horn in on my date," he whispered. He revved the outboard motor and glared at me with fire in his eyes.

The wind whipped my hair around, and I could see my face reflected in the mirrored lenses of Doug's sunglasses. "I wouldn't worry too much about that," I whispered, gesturing at his shades. "Who could refuse a guy with those slick sunglasses? You look like you came right out of an American action movie."

"Watch it, Viper!" Doug warned.

"Will you two stop fighting?" Aiby said from the

bow of the boat. She had one leg overboard and the other leaning on the picnic basket Doug had lovingly prepared for the two of them.

Aiby watched the water. I could tell she was worried, but I didn't know if it was because the tower idea seemed dangerous or because we still needed to find Cumai's brother and appease the Others' wrath. I still didn't understand everything that had happened, nor why Semueld Askell was to blame.

Doug had closed himself off in grumpy silence, his muscles flexing under his shirt as he corrected our course over the waves.

Patches was so excited he couldn't sit still. He alternated between being the perfect figurehead — paws outside the bow and ears in the wind — and curling up around the picnic basket in the back.

I kept quiet, trying to put my thoughts into order. *So much for the idea of a relaxing summer,* I thought.

I thought about the bonfire on the hill, and I told myself that more or less all the men in the village had to be aware of its "magical" meaning, even though they didn't talk about it. I remembered my father's advice and the coin I'd found in the lining of my grandfather's jacket. I tried to remember the gestures Prospero had

made during the funeral, wondering which of them were used to communicate with the inhabitants of the Hollow World.

I also thought about the Borderpassers and wondered who could have gone into Cumai's mill after she was dead. Since you had to be a Borderpasser to enter her place, whoever had found her body had to be one, too. Where had Cumai been buried? I hadn't looked for it, but I was certain there wasn't a freshly dug grave in the church's cemetery.

Was this mystery was linked to Reverend Prospero's disappearance?

And how did the Ark of the Passages play into things?

Thousands of questions like these circled in my head, but one, in particular, kept coming back to haunt me. As I looked at Aiby's black hair flowing in the wind, I wondered if there was a magical object that could make me six months older and six inches taller.

* * *

We arrived at the Sheir Thraid reef when the sun was high in the middle of the sky — at least as bright as it could get in Scotland. Doug slowed the motor to an idle and leaned over to check the sea floor. Stretches

of clear, shallow water alternated with ominously dark, blue pools.

"Did you hear about Reverend Prospero?" my brother asked after going halfway around the reef, and then steering the boat toward it.

I shook my head. "He wasn't in the rectory this morning," I said. "Do you know what happened to him?"

"Who knows," Doug said, turning off the motor and letting the current slowly push us toward the shore. "Aiby, can you pull the anchor out from under there? Just toss it out and it should hold."

Aiby took the small anchor attached to a chain and threw it into the sea with a *plop!*

Doug reached into the picnic basket. Without saying anything to Aiby, he opened a can of soda. "This morning, Piper told me the Reverend went out last night to bury Cumai at sea," he said. He took a long gulp, then added, "But he never came back."

Aiby was standing and examining the tower with her hands on her hips. She seemed to be gauging the risks involved in jumping off the top. "What do you mean he didn't come back?" Aiby asked without glancing back at either of us.

Doug shrugged. "No one saw him return."

"But he went out to sea with some other men," I pointed out.

"Yeah," Doug said. "McStay, Everett, and McBlack went with him. So what?"

"None of them said where he was?" I asked.

Doug looked at me stubbornly. "That's what I said," he said, which he hadn't actually said. Then he looked at the reef and asked, "So we're here. Now what?"

From around sixty-five feet away, the cliff seemed little more than a big rock poking out of the surface of the water. The tower itself looked like a huge thermometer, or a giant harpoon that had been driven into the back of a giant whale. It was seventy-five feet high, give or take a few feet.

"Let's go up," Aiby said.

"You're crazy," Doug said.

Aiby smiled at him. "Don't tell anyone, okay?" she joked.

Aiby took off her plaid shirt and slipped off her jeans. Without another word, she dove into water, leaving the image of her red swimsuit burned into my retinas.

I slipped my T-shirt off and wrapped it around the scorpion key I'd removed from my neck. I hesitated at the edge of the boat, wondering how cold the water was.

"Hey, Viper! You're in great shape — for a skeleton," Doug said. He flexed his rugby-player muscles and smirked at me.

I ignored him and jumped into the water. Patches let out a worried whine, but didn't follow.

Chapter
ELEVEN

CLIMBING, WAITING, & JUMPING

The water in the North Sea was never all that warm, even in the summer, but as a man of the north, I was used to it. All the same, when I hit the water, my toes bunched up, my stomach clenched, and I felt the familiar sensation of goose bumps crowding my flesh. I burst through the surface and filled my lungs.

I spotted Aiby's head above the water and followed her, doing the doggie-paddle so I could keep track of my distance from the reef below us. Much of the coast around Applecross was covered with gravel, but wherever shoals and reefs sprang up, towers like this one marked them. In some places, the sea floor was so deep that a submarine couldn't even reach it.

As we swam, the blood in my veins began to warm.

Schools of silvery fish darted below me. The undertow slammed me from one place to another, so I had to be careful to push off from the rock protrusions with my hands. After fifteen strokes I was nearly scraping the rock with my stomach. I got to my feet.

Aiby was several feet in front of me, moving with the agility of some sort of mystical sea monkey. She waited for the wave to crest, then balanced herself on her long legs and hopped from one stone to another. From there, she stretched out an arm until she could almost touch the wooden base of the signal tower. It had once been painted red and white, but the sun, wind, and salt had almost completely removed any color.

I watched as Aiby slipped a foot between the planks and pulled herself up, sticking to the tower like a spider in a web of wooden supports. I followed her, my cold gym shorts glued to my skin, dripping seawater.

"This way!" she said without even looking at me. "It should be up there."

I didn't know what she was talking about or how she could even know the structure of an old tower on a reef that she'd never seen before. But I climbed after her, grabbing the first of the cross-shaped boards and pulling myself up. I felt an encouraging wave of satisfaction. If there was one thing I was good at, it was climbing. Barn

rooftops, trees, or signal towers, it mattered little — I could climb them all. I was skinny and weighed almost nothing, but strong enough that I could pull myself up with the fingers of one hand.

I climbed quickly — more quickly than Aiby, even. She was moving like a rock climber, her stomach pressed against the wood with at least two safe holds before reaching for a new one. I, on the other hand, climbed guided by animal instinct. I chose my handholds along the boards at the last minute, blindly relying on them.

I had almost reached the top when a piece of wood crumbled into a burst of splinters in my hand. I found myself connected to the tower by only my left hand, swinging fifteen feet above the bare rock of the reef, my legs dangling precariously. If I fell, the best possible outcome would be a broken leg.

I saw Doug below us, firmly gripping his binoculars. He might've been checking to make sure nothing bad happened to me, but knowing my brother, I figured he was aiming them at Aiby's butt at the highest magnification possible.

I grunted and pulled myself up with the only hand that still had a firm grip. Another two grabs and I could see the wooden cage and the platform at the top. A beacon in the center could be lit to mark the presence

of the reef during a storm. Aiby caught up with me, then we both squeezed through the bars. Her hair was shimmering from the water and her green eyes matched the color of the waves below us. She looked like a wild jungle creature accustomed to climbing trees. I felt like a land mammal trapped seventy-five feet above the ground.

Below us, my dog was running from one side of the boat to the other, as if trying to find the courage to dive in and follow me. Doug lowered his binoculars and bent over to pet Patches, trying to calm him. "Relax, old boy," Doug said, handing my dog a tuna sandwich. "Those two will be back soon."

I glanced out over the horizon. I could see all the way to the village. I recognized the little church and the post office, the dark-roofed cottages, and the old mill. There was the winding route of the Baelanch Ba — the oxen road — where it split and headed into Applecross. The other path led up into the mountains, which were completely covered by clouds.

I circled the tower. On the other side, the clouds were tangled up with the island of Skyle. Some gulls had taken flight near the coast, curious about our presence. The sea splashed below us in chaotic fashion, currents crossing each other in ominous whirlpools. At times, the rows of

rock at the surface looked like a whale's backbone.

Aiby was scratching away the salt deposits on one of the railings, seemingly looking for something. "Here it is," she said, clinging to me. In the narrow space of the cage, I felt her wet skin press against mine. Even though I was careful to brush against her as little as possible, her hair kept brushing my neck.

Aiby was pointing to something carved into the wood. It was written in the Enchanted Language. I was so astonished by this fact that, incredibly, I managed to read it. "Tame the Leap of Magic," I said.

"The *Time* for the Leap of Magic," Aiby said, correcting me.

Well, I'd almost read it.

"Time is this place, Fin," Aiby whispered. "And Magic is the sea down there below. It's what surrounds us and hides us. Time and Magic are two sides of the same coin . . . like two things no longer able to be separated."

Aiby faced me, her amazing green eyes six inches above my nose. I thought that Time had stopped high above the reef, and Magic was the distance separating our eyelashes. It felt infinite and immediate all at once.

Somehow we'd gotten even closer to each other. The tip of my nose was touching hers.

With her pressed next to me, it did feel like we were

inseparable. And at that moment, for some strange reason I still don't understand, I remembered the coin with two heads that I'd found in my jacket during Cumai's funeral.

"My grandfather!" I suddenly exclaimed.

Aiby recoiled, bumping her head against the cage and pushing me away. She glared at me, the wind lifting her hair into the air so that it looked like snakes. "What are you talking about?" she asked.

I felt cold prickling across the surface of my exposed skin. I wasn't sure what to say just yet, so I said nothing.

"In any case," she growled, "it's here at the top, Finley McPhee, that you can find out if you're a Borderpasser or not."

"Huh?" I asked her, completely confused — by her, the world, and myself. What had made me think of my grandfather right then?

Aiby pointed toward the waves, but I couldn't focus. I felt overwhelmed by my stupidity. I peered out over the edge of the signal tower, keeping my balance. Down in the boat below us, my brother began waving his arms for me to climb down.

He was probably right. No matter where I looked, all I saw were the chaotic waves and endless expanse of the cloud-filled sky.

Mr. Lily had said magic happens when you believe it's real. That it happens when you want it to be real. I'd been a fraction of an inch from kissing Aiby and I had completely ruined it. I remembered the Second Chance Watch I'd been given, but it was wrapped in my shirt in the boat. I wished I could use it to take me back in time to when my nose was touching Aiby's.

Would I even get a second chance to kiss her? Or was that a once in a lifetime opportunity? I sighed.

"Finley McPhee?" Aiby said. "Are you okay?"

I snapped to, remembering I'd climbed up there to find out if I was a Borderpasser or not. Aiby looked frightened, as if she no longer thought I should take the leap of faith. I just smiled at her.

"Finley, if you don't feel up to this, you need to climb back down right away," Aiby said.

Of course I didn't feel up to it. I *couldn't* feel up to doing something like that. Diving from that signal tower was more or less like throwing yourself off the third floor of a building . . . or like flying off a bicycle over a curve on the coastal road. The last time I'd done something like that, I had died and spent an extraordinary night inside a tree, playing cards with a magical creature.

Time and Magic.

A coin with two heads.

One male and one female.

I spread my arms wide. The wind, my friends, only speaks to madmen — and I heard it call my name.

I jumped.

"Finley!" Aiby screamed. Her hand brushed against my feet.

"FINLEY!" Doug yelled.

Patches barked loudly.

It was a fast drop.

I curled into a ball. I heard someone scream. I saw that Patches had finally found the courage to fling himself off the boat.

I closed my eyes and fell to pieces, like I'd dived into a mirror and shattered.

At first it hurt. The splinters began to sting. The wounds began to ooze sap. The sap thickened, running warm in my frozen veins.

I opened my eyes and found myself in silent darkness. But it was like the silence before a play begins, one brief moment before the curtain rises.

I waited.

Flashes of light flickered above me. I turned and saw the sky and the clouds passing by. They were moving fast while I remained motionless.

I saw the sea foam. I saw the exact spot where the

rocks cut through the water, making it frothy. Bubbles of oxygen spread in all directions like pollen from a submerged flower. I floated, caught in a stasis that seemed to last an eternity.

I glimpsed a flash below me. Then another.

I turned again, and this time I saw the yardarm of an old ship, the wrecked and sunken carcass of a wooden relic. I touched something with the tip of my toe. I'd reached the bottom of the sea. I'd fallen thirty feet below the water's surface, or maybe a mile. Impossible to tell.

The flash that had called to me was coming from an old coin. There were lots of them scattered across the sea bottom near a partly open trunk that had been swallowed up by algae.

The coins had no tails and two heads, the cargo of an ancient ship that had broken up along the reef and never returned.

Like Reginald Lily, I thought. *Like the Reverend, maybe.*

I took one, two coins. I took three. I grabbed a handful. I grasped them with my fingers and felt a pang in my heart. My head beat like a drum.

I was out of air.

Aiby, I thought.

I fluttered my legs and ascended, my eyes open as I aimed toward the shards of sky. The passing of clouds.

The passages.

I swam with only my legs, like a fish, and I rose.

I rose.

The air hit me like a slap.

I opened my mouth wide and gasped. The oxygen filled my lungs like it was electric.

"Patches!" I cried out.

He was swimming very poorly and his ears floated on top of the water like little furry creatures. All he could do was jump on my head and lick my face.

"Cut it out, buddy!" I cried. "You'll drown me!"

I grabbed him by the collar and he clung to me. Somehow I began swimming toward the boat. I saw Aiby's legs running along the reef. My vision was blurry.

I coughed furiously as my brother pulled me onboard, grabbing me by my gym shorts.

"A stupid brother!" he kept repeating. "That's what I have — a stupid brother!"

I fell into the bottom of the boat and burst out laughing. The boat tilted as Aiby climbed in with Patches behind her. He jumped on top of me and licked my face.

I closed my eyes and opened them up again. "So?" I asked Aiby, who I found sitting next to me. "Am I a Borderpasser?"

This time, she smiled. "You are," she replied.

"Of course you are," Doug growled. "How else do you think you survived that?"

He pulled up the anchor and turned on the motor. I closed my eyes and opened them again, petting Patches.

I saw a gleam in the bottom of the boat. I stretched out my hand and grabbed a coin. Had I managed to bring one up from the bottom of the sea? Or was it the one I'd thrown from the hill on the night of the funeral? Had it landed in the boat docked below, totally by chance? That seemed unlikely.

But it *was* possible.

Anything was possible.

After all . . . I'm a Borderpasser.

Chapter
TWELVE

THE STREAM,
THE MILL, &
THE KEY

All the lights were still lit at Cumai's mill. They filtered through the closed shutters in the dark, making the mill look spooky to say the least. The old stone house had never seemed intimidating to me before. I'd passed by it many times, practically every one of the seventy mornings of school that I'd skipped to go fishing. The same seventy mornings that had caused me to flunk the school year.

The building was on the north side of town, perched on the riverbank like a tortoise made of white stone. It had no name. To us it was just "the old mill," or "Cumai's mill." The river, however, was called the Calghorn Dinn, which meant "stinky puddle" in the language of the Little People. And I had spent many spring mornings along the banks of one of those puddles, fishing.

By the time we got there, it was already the middle of the afternoon. Doug stopped the boat a little bit upstream of where the river flowed into the sea, passing around a rock that was bigger than the rest. Before letting us step onto land, he warned us, "Either you tell me now what just happened or I'll go to your parents and tell them everything."

"You mean *our* parents, Doug?" I teased.

"Don't try to be smart with me, Viper," he said.

"I'm not trying to be smart," I argued.

"Oh, yeah?" he erupted. "Then what do you call the ravens from last night? And what were you doing today at the tower? Testing your courage? You're up to something."

"Something, yes," I admitted. "And I'm very sorry I involved you, but there wasn't any other way to get to Sheir Thraid."

Doug didn't back off at all. "That goes for you, too, Aiby! No stories about picnics, giants, or I don't know what. Not this time. I want the truth."

"I'll do what I can, Doug," Aiby said.

"Then explain to me why we have to go into the house of someone who just died," he said.

"Why *do* we need to go in there now?" I asked. "To turn off the lights, perhaps?"

110

Aiby gave me a dirty look. Before Doug could respond, she clarified, "We have to go look for a clue about Cumai's brother."

"What brother?" Doug insisted.

"Listen," I stepped in. "Please just wait for us here, Doug."

"Fat chance!" he shouted.

"Or at the pond," I suggested. "It's just for a minute. Go north from here until you get to the oak skull. Ignore the sign warning you to turn back. Then go one hundred or so steps farther. Your fishing rod is hidden in the hollow of the tree that was struck by lightning. There should also be some flies there so you can fish for a while."

"My fishing rod?" Doug roared. "*My* fishing rod, Finley?!"

I'd made a mistake. A *big* one.

A while ago, I'd swiped Doug's Deep Sea Victory fishing pole. When he'd been trying to prove I'd stolen it at the beginning of the summer, I'd narrowly managed to get to the pond just before he did to hide it. Ever since, I'd been waiting for things to calm down before putting the Victory back in its rightful place in Doug's room.

I needed to change the subject quickly. "Okay," I said. "Come to the mill with us and I'll explain everything."

Surprised by my change in attitude, Doug froze like a deer in the headlights of a car. In silence, he followed us toward old lady Cumai's house. Patches trotted happily along at our feet.

The mill was silent. I couldn't help but notice the glimmer of the electric lights sneaking through the blinds. I forced myself to examine the building.

Look, Finley, I thought. *Look carefully.*

The mill consisted of two floors and a dark thatched roof. The water in the stream was gurgling into many small pools that reflected the blue sky. The longer I looked, the more dense the tall shadows grew. Perfect for going to look for missing brothers and murderers.

We reached the wooden front door. It rested atop a massive stone doorstep. It was locked.

"Now what?" Doug asked.

"Somerled gave us the key," I said.

"And who's Somerled?" he asked.

"McBlack's daughter," I said.

"So why did McBlack's daughter have the key to Cumai's mill?" he asked.

"Actually, that's a good question," I admitted. "See, we have to go into the old mill because we think old lady Cumai was murdered."

"Murdered? She was eighty years old," Doug said. "And why? A crime of passion by her jealous, hundred-year-old secret lover?"

"That's not funny, Doug," Aiby said. "Cumai really was murdered."

"Then who did it?" he asked.

"Semueld Askell," she said.

Doug considered that for a moment. "I don't know who that is."

"He's a dangerous visitor who's hiding in the village," Aiby said.

Doug snorted. "And he came all the way here to murder little old ladies?"

"Cumai wasn't a normal old lady," Aiby said.

"I agree with you," Doug said. "She was a batty old lady."

"Askell is a kinkishin," I said, realizing the conversation was going nowhere.

"A what?" Doug asked.

"Someone who knows how to use Sidhe Strikes, I said. "They're heart attacks. That's how she was killed, with a Sidhe Strike."

"Okay," my brother said. He remained silent for a long time before saying, "You're pulling my leg."

"I've never been more serious in my life," I said.

Aiby nodded. To convince Doug, she pulled the wooden key out of my backpack, slipped it into the door's keyhole, and then paused. "Stay back, you two. Especially you," she said to Doug.

"Why especially me?" my brother asked. "Are there any more surprises?"

"There might be," I said.

Aiby turned the key. One, two, three times. Five times. Ten times. It kept turning and turning but didn't catch the locking mechanism.

Aiby stopped after turning it at least twenty times. "I think something isn't working," she said. She banged on the door, but it stayed firmly locked. She pulled the key out of the keyhole and slid it in a second time. She tried again, but no change. She passed it to me and I gave it a shot, but the results were identical.

"Maybe she gave you the wrong key," Doug said. "Here, let me give it a try."

I shrugged and handed him the key. Doug spun it around and around in the lock while Aiby and I circled the perimeter of the mill in search of a side entrance. We found nothing. The ground floor of the old house had only one entrance, which Doug was snorting in front of like an angry bull.

MAP OF THE PASSAGES

"Do you hear that?" I said. "Listen." Two audible clicks sounded with every turn of the key. "It clicks twice with each revolution, but nothing happens."

"Maybe it's a Magical Threshold like the one at the Emporium," Aiby said, bending over to feel the stone at the bottom of the door. "Maybe we can't get in because it doesn't recognize us, or because we're missing something."

Aiby told me to turn around. She dug through my backpack, pulled out a case, and opened it. In it was a pair of glasses kind of like the ones that Meb had shown me that morning. However, on both sides of these glasses was a selection of colored filters that could be snapped into place in front of the lenses. There were seven sets, one for each color of the rainbow. Aiby put them on and immediately her face took on an expression of deep concentration.

"Hey, those make you look like a movie star," I joked.

"Never underestimate the Fludd Lenses," Aiby mumbled. She chose the violet filter and quickly used it to examine the stone doorstep. "There is magic here." She rapidly changed filters, moving to the orange one. "And I'd say it's the Voice of Friends."

"Ah-ha! Now everything's as clear as a glass of ink on a dark and moonless night," I joked.

Aiby glared at me from behind the colored lenses. "Excuse me?"

I turned red. "Sorry," I said. "It just came out of me without warning."

She sighed. "Anyway, now we know this needs to be opened magically."

"Like with a two-headed coin?" I asked.

"That's a Borderpassing coin," Aiby said, as if speaking about the most normal thing in the world.

"You getting any of this?" I asked Doug.

Doug scratched his neck. "Um," he said. I could always count on Doug to be just as confused as I was, if not more so, when it came to magical things. "The most magical method of opening locks that I know of is to call the locksmith."

"Or my father," Aiby muttered, slipping off the Fludd Lenses.

I turned toward the sea and watched the waves, quiet and calm. My still-wet hair made me think back to my dive and the coin with two heads. I turned back to face the door and tried turning the key while clutching the coin. I put the coin on top of the key and placed it on the doorstep. The lock just kept turning in circles.

"We'll be here all night," Doug grumbled. "And I have to go back to the farm to help Dad soon."

Aiby made one last attempt, trying all the different lenses again while putting the key into the lock very carefully. She seemed to be looking for an unusual mechanism or special contact point that would make the mechanism release, but nothing worked.

A wooden door. An iron lock. A wooden key. The solution had to be something simple, because I couldn't see a slightly crazy old lady carrying out a complicated routine every time she wanted to get inside her own house.

I couldn't even remember ever seeing the door open or close. Cumai always seemed to be either outside or inside whenever I'd passed by.

I leaned over the river and focused on the mill mirrored in the pool of water.

Think, Finley, I thought. *Reflect. How might a magic door to a mill be opened?*

With a special word, I realized with dismay. It could be any word in the world. Or the other world, too.

"How do you say 'open up' in the Enchanted Language?" I asked.

Aiby tilted her head. She tried turning the key while saying, "Recluditur!"

Then Doug tried, and failed. I saw both of them mirrored in the river.

Maybe it's not a magical door to a normal mill, I thought. *Maybe it's a normal door to a mill that a magical being lived in.*

Which didn't solve the problem at all, but rather reversed it.

"What if we do it backward?" I asked Aiby. "Did you try turning it the other way already?"

"Of course!" they both answered. "And that didn't change anything," Aiby added.

"Not in reverse," I mumbled without looking away from the river. "Well, not exactly in reverse, but more like . . ."

Doug stared at me. "Well?" he asked, growing impatient.

The hair on the back of my neck stood up. "Doug?" I said.

"What?" he asked.

"Can you bring me the key?" I asked.

"Where?"

"Here. Right where I am," I said.

"What? Why?" Doug asked.

"Can you please just bring me the key?" I asked.

Aiby passed it to him, and in the blink of an eye Doug was standing next to me. When I stretched out my hand to take the key, the hair on my arm stood up, too.

"Do you notice something weird about this stream?" I asked my brother.

"Like what?" he asked.

"Look at the reflection of the mill," I said.

Doug began to inspect the pools of water from the river. After a couple of seconds, he grabbed my wrist. "Whoa," he whispered.

"Exactly," I whispered back. "The mill that's mirrored in the river has all its windows open, and —"

"And there's someone looking out the window at us!" Doug said, finishing my thought.

We both looked up at the window in the middle of the second floor, but there was no one looking back at us. The shutters were closed.

"Let's go home, okay?" Doug said, his voice shakier than I'd ever heard it.

"The door isn't what's magic here," I said to Aiby. "It's the mill. It's this whole place."

"I bet it was built on an Indian burial ground or something," Doug said, as if there could've been an Indian burial ground in Scotland, though I had to admit I'd been thinking something similar. "We need Reverend Prospero," Doug added. "We need him here."

I don't know why, but I was suddenly reminded

of my image in the mirror that morning. I'd looked at myself and asked, *So what will happen today?* And then I'd brushed my teeth while watching myself in the mirror.

I took a step away from both Aiby and Doug, held out the wooden key as if it were a toothbrush, and approached the water. Carefully, I tried to match the reflection of the key to the reflection of the door.

The reflection of the lock on the surface of the water was tiny. The pool was rippling a little, but I managed to guide the key into the hole. I heard a *click!* come from the actual door to the mill.

"Finley?" Aiby said.

I turned the key in the air. The reflection in the river turned along with it, and the door to the mill let out a second *click!*

"Finley?" Aiby said a little louder.

Finally, with a third turn and a third *click!*, the door to Cumai's mill opened. I dropped the wooden key to the ground, inexplicably exhausted from the effort.

"Wow!" said Doug. "You really are a magician, Viper. Who would've thought?"

"How did you think of that?" Aiby asked. Her look seemed like one of admiration, which caught me completely off guard.

I shrugged and smirked. "I reflected on it," I said simply.

Aiby rolled her eyes, and we went inside.

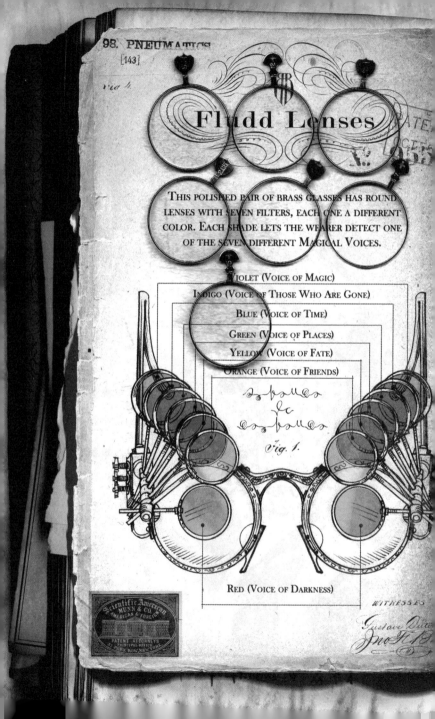

Fludd Lenses

THIS POLISHED PAIR OF BRASS GLASSES HAS ROUND
LENSES WITH SEVEN FILTERS, EACH ONE A DIFFERENT
COLOR. EACH SHADE LETS THE WEARER DETECT ONE
OF THE SEVEN DIFFERENT MAGICAL VOICES.

VIOLET (VOICE OF MAGIC)

INDIGO (VOICE OF THOSE WHO ARE GONE)

BLUE (VOICE OF TIME)

GREEN (VOICE OF PLACES)

YELLOW (VOICE OF FATE)

ORANGE (VOICE OF FRIENDS)

Fig. 1.

RED (VOICE OF DARKNESS)

WITNESSES

Chapter
THIRTEEN

A CLOISTER, AN APPLE TREE, & FIRE

It was completely silent inside the mill. The fragrance of herbs, lavender, foxglove, and aromatic spices wafted through the air. The electric lights vibrated softly and gave off heat from days of running constantly. I turned off all the lights by gently flipping the switches. With each light turned off, it felt more and more like I was taking care of the place.

We passed a small hallway with some stairs heading up to the second floor and found ourselves in a large kitchen. The mid-afternoon light flickered vibrantly through the closed shutters. Parsnips, zucchini, and potatoes were halfway sliced atop a cutting board. Copper pots hung along the white walls. An old refrigerator hummed faintly in a corner.

123

As I moved through the rooms, the house started to seem like it'd been left only a few hours prior. The kitchen's second door was open, which led to an inner cloister very much like a courtyard. An array of columns and small archways surrounded the lawn, with a little vegetable garden highlighted by a skylight. In the center of the lawn was a large apple tree. Its branches filled much of the space. A few words were written on the white marble threshold in the Enchanted Language:

HINC NON POSSIS IRE

Aiby used the violet lenses in her glasses to examine it. "It's a Glyph of Protection," she said. "With a strong Voice of Magic."

I nodded, pretending to completely understand what all that meant while wondering if Aiby would fall for it. She passed her fingers over the letters and said, "It's a very ancient dialect. I can't figure out what it says."

Obviously, the letters were incomprehensible to me, as well. "Do you want me to ask Doug?" I said.

My brother had just picked up the lid from one of the pots that had been left on the stove. He immediately put it back down with a disgusted look. "Someone needs to come and clean this up as soon as possible."

I showed him the marble doorstep Aiby was leaning over. "What do you make of this?" I asked.

Doug's eyebrows pinched together. "Why do you two want to enter a closet?" he asked.

"Wait — what?" I asked.

"It's a closet," Doug said, pointing to the wide-open door of the cloister.

Aiby lightly touched my shoulder, which was just enough to make me realize that Doug couldn't see it. He wasn't a Borderpasser like we were.

"A closet, of course," I said, and then nodded. "Perhaps while Aiby and I check what's inside this closet, you could search the other rooms?"

"Okay," he said. "But what should I be looking for?"

"Photos, diaries, appointments — anything that can help us figure out who Cumai's brother is or where he might be," Aiby said.

My brother nodded and headed off.

"And Doug?" I said as he was leaving the kitchen.

"What is it now, Viper?"

"Watch out for the, um, closets," I said.

Doug rolled his eyes at me and left.

With Doug gone, Aiby crossed the magical threshold, then turned and held out her hand to me. As my fingers joined hers, I could feel her skin vibrate.

Together, we entered Cumai's magical cloister. If I had to describe what it felt like, I'd say it was like getting

goose bumps, the heebie-jeebies, and the willies all at the same time.

While it was a peaceful place, it was clear it'd recently been broken into. In the magical stillness, the apple tree in the middle seemed more like a sculpture than a living thing. In one corner were two straw cushions that had been thrown onto the ground. Nearby was an upended table and some overturned bowls. When we got closer, I noticed a sewing basket with spools of thread, needles, and balls of wool scattered all around it. A rocking chair was tilted forward with its back resting unnaturally on the edge of a stone fireplace. The fire had recently gone out, judging by the glowing embers.

Aiby looked around cautiously, alternating between the various colored filters of the Fludd Lenses. I slipped between the columns to get a better look at the little vegetable garden in the middle. The apple tree stood out against the vegetables and fragrant flowers. It was a real-life secret garden if I'd ever seen one.

Aiby called me over. She turned me around and pulled something from my backpack — this time it was an amber pouch with the words *Remember Embers* written on it.

"Let's see if they still work," she said. She stooped down in front of the fireplace, stirred the ashes with a

126

stick, and then blew on the embers. As soon as she saw they were glowing again, she poured the contents of the pouch over them. "Stand back," she warned, quickly getting to her feet.

The fire in the fireplace burst to life as a black, flickering flame leapt out from the embers. Eerie shapes danced in the flames.

Patches barked. Aiby quickly changed the colored lenses in her glasses from orange to indigo. She bent down, so I followed suit. The black flames in the fireplace flickered until they transformed themselves into dark figures like you might see in a shadow puppet theater. I saw a man with a hooked nose pass by, wearing a strange cloak. I immediately recognized him as Semueld Askell.

"The shapes in the flames are showing the events that took place in front of the fireplace before it went out," Aiby explained.

It was then that I finally understood a detail in Somerled's story. She had mentioned hearing the noise of someone who made a clinking noise in the cloister. I figured it'd end up being a woman wearing heels, but I was wrong. The noise had to have come from the tinkling mirrors on Askell's magical cloak.

Semueld's shadow passed in front of the fireplace a second time, and then a third, as if Askell had been

pacing back and forth without stopping. Next to him, I recognized the outline of old lady Cumai. The two shadows came close to each other, waving their arms around in fierce argument. Cumai shoved Askell, whose cloak came undone after getting caught on something. He tugged on it violently to free it.

I watched the black flames, trying to imagine the conversation occurring during this silent replay. Aiby took my hand and squeezed, and I realized that we were about to see a reenactment of Cumai's murder.

Just then, the argument between Askell and Cumai calmed down as the two turned away from each other. Cumai's shadow exited the scene via the left side of the fireplace. Askell, however, quickly produced a tiny cylinder from inside his cloak, brought it to his lips, and blew into it.

"A blowgun!" I exclaimed. "He used a blowgun!"

Aiby covered her mouth with both hands and went even paler than normal. "That's how he used the Sidhe Strike," she murmured.

We watched Askell's shadow blow into the tube a second time, then conceal the blowgun back beneath his cloak. With that, the embers and shadows vanished, leaving behind a pile of lifeless gray soot.

We got up slowly, looking around to see where Cumai had been found after the Sidhe Strike struck her. Aiby changed the lenses on the glasses from indigo to red. She examined the rocking chair, the table, and the spools of thread scattered on the ground. I stayed where I was, contemplating the macabre scene that took place not long before in front of this very hearth.

I moved away from the basket of firewood and saw a tiny flash of light on the ground. I reached down and picked up a shard from Askell's Cloak of Mirrors.

"Aiby," I called. "I found something."

"Come here," she said. "I found something, too."

"Better than a shard from Askell's cloak?"

"Maybe," Aiby said.

I joined her. Aiby was holding a silver arrow the size of the tip of a ballpoint pen.

"Apparently Askell missed with one of his two darts," Aiby said. She pointed to my backpack again. "You should have some Essential Pouches in there. Let's put these things inside one so we can ask my dad about them later."

"Maybe we aren't the right ones to be doing this," I said. "I mean, we aren't exactly trained for it."

"Oh?" Aiby said. "Do you know a Magical Detective?"

129

I squinted at her. "They exist?" I asked.

"I know two of them," Aiby said. "Professor Bell and Edgar Allan. Three, if we include Edgar's raven. But I don't think any of them can help us at the moment."

"They live too far away?" I ventured.

"No, but they have been dead for more than a century," Aiby said, holding up the arrow between her fingers.

We had just placed the arrow and the shard of mirror safely into separate pouches when I heard Doug's alarmed voice from just outside the kitchen door.

"Finley, Aiby!" said, somewhere between a whisper and a scream. "There's someone outside!"

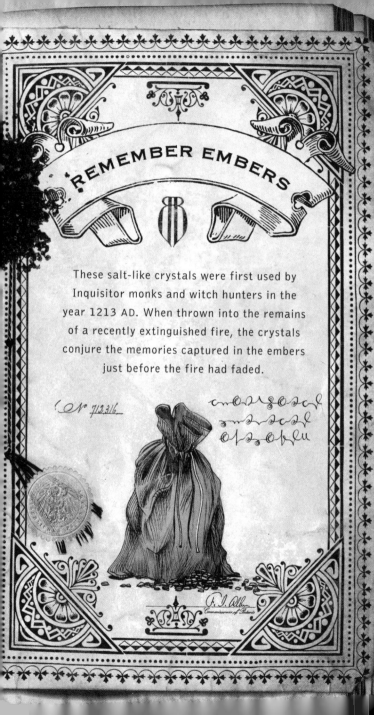

REMEMBER EMBERS

These salt-like crystals were first used by Inquisitor monks and witch hunters in the year 1213 AD. When thrown into the remains of a recently extinguished fire, the crystals conjure the memories captured in the embers just before the fire had faded.

N° 7/23/16

Chapter
FOURTEEN

INTRUDERS,
BUSYBODIES, &
RUNNERS

We hid in the kitchen amongst the shadows. Doug was perplexed by the way we'd suddenly materialized out of the closet, but he said nothing. Patches growled softly and aimed his snout at the window like a pointer. Aiby was still wearing those ridiculous glasses with the colored lenses.

I listened to the footsteps outside the mill with a fair amount of anxiety. The intruder stopped in front of the entrance, cleaned off his shoes with something, and then rested a hand on the half-open door. Patches tilted his head and wagged his tail.

The intruder gently pushed on the door and took a single step inside. "Is anyone there?" a masculine voice asked — one that I knew I should recognize.

"Is someone there?" the man at the door repeated, coming a step closer.

Doug mouthed a name: *Mr. Everett.*

I nodded in agreement. "Professor Everett?" I said. "Is that you?"

The person outside the door hesitated a moment. "McPhee?" he said. "Is that Finley? Are you inside?"

"I'm in the kitchen, Mr. Everett," I said.

"I'm here, too," Doug said.

"Hello," Aiby added.

Professor Everett came into the kitchen, closing the door behind him. In his hand was a walking stick with a carved duck's beak for a handle.

"What are you three doing here?" he asked, eyebrows raised. "You gave me quite a fright."

"We might ask you the same question," I said, surprised by my own courage.

Mr. Everett took a couple of hesitant steps toward us while leaning on the walking stick. He seemed to use it more out of habit than real necessity. When he got to the table in the middle of the kitchen, I couldn't help but notice the long knife that still lay there amidst the abandoned vegetables.

Professor Everett let out a deep sigh. "This story gets stranger every day," he said.

"Agreed," Aiby muttered.

Mr. Everett pulled one of the cane chairs out and sat down, leaning his head on his hands. He locked eyes with my brother. "What are you doing here, Doug?" he said. "Shouldn't you be working on the farm with your father right now?"

Doug was caught off guard by the accusation, which was probably Mr. Everett's intent. "Oh, I let him know I needed a couple hours off to . . . to go on a picnic," Doug said, flushing red.

Aiby smiled. "What about you, Mr. Everett? To put it frankly — what are *you* doing here?"

He leaned in close to the three of us. "Frankly, you say? All right then, my child, I'll tell you frankly why I'm here: I was somewhat of a friend to Cumai. In fact, I was a very close friend. I came to see her every week and brought her things from the shop," Mr. Everett said. He waved his hands at the space around us. "And whenever it was possible, we spent several hours sitting right here and chatting about old times." He sighed. "And besides, I'm the one who found her." He pointed to the white doorstep that led to the secret cloister, the one that Doug saw as a simple closet. "Right there, resting on that . . ."

I waited to hear which word he'd choose to describe the magical door.

Doug spoke instead, ruining my plan. "In front of the closet," Doug said.

Mr. Everett nodded. "Yes, my good boy. The closet."

I exchanged looks with Aiby. She was clutching the Fludd Lenses in her fist.

"It was a terrible thing," Mr. Everett added, "and entirely unexpected. After finding her dead, I went to get help. I've only now had time to return to clean up her place since no one else will do it."

"She had a brother," I said.

"A brother, you say?" he asked. The expression on his face was one of surprise, though his voice was flat. "I'm fairly certain she didn't have a brother."

"Come on, Mr. Everett," Aiby said. "We said we'd talk about things frankly. If you really were Cumai's friend, I find it unlikely that she never mentioned her brother to you. The one who lives on the islands."

"The guardian," I added.

With those few words, Mr. Everett's face soured. His fingers stiffened as if he were grabbing some invisible object from the air. "But *you* shouldn't know about him," he said, pausing to collect his thoughts. "Ah, but, of course! It was your father, right? It had to have been your father."

Mr. Everett was looking at Aiby, so I figured he must be referring to Locan Lily.

"So will you tell us what really happened here, Mr. Everett?" Aiby said, her voice impressively calm considering the circumstances.

Mr. Everett's eyes darted around as quickly as a ferret. It reminded me of my friend Sammy when he cheated on his homework and got caught — an unmistakable blend of anger and guilt.

"Oh, well, it's a very complicated matter," Mr. Everett said.

"I can imagine," Aiby said. "But perhaps I can explain it to you."

"You shouldn't be able to explain anything at all," Mr. Everett muttered. "But certainly, if you know about her brother, then you also know about last night."

"Of course," I said. "We also know about the Reverend."

Mr. Everett's eyes grew large. "I see," he said. "And if you know about the Reverend, then you'll understand why I came here: we divided up the work, so to speak."

"*Who* divided up *what* work?" Aiby asked.

"Those who were with him at the funeral," Mr. Everett said. "To protect him and to convince *them!*"

137

That's when everything came together. Mr. Lily's story about the Others who were infuriated by Cumai's death, Doug's story about the funeral at sea that the Reverend hadn't returned from, and Somerled's story about what had happened inside the mill. Just like that, all became clear to me.

The short tale that followed confirmed it. Apparently Mr. Everett, Reverend Prospero, Mr. McBlack, Mr. McStay, and Piper had left via boat a little after midnight, telling the others they were going to bury old lady Cumai at sea as she'd requested.

"But in reality, we weren't supposed to bury her at sea," Mr. Everett confessed. "We were supposed to . . . deliver her."

"*Return* her," Aiby corrected him. Once again Mr. Everett was surprised by what we knew about the situation.

"Yes," he admitted with difficulty. "We were supposed to return her to the Others. We were supposed to bring her to one of the islands, following a course that only the Reverend knew, and deliver her to her brother. But when we got there, things didn't go well. There were so many people on that island. People whom none of us had ever seen before. Not even the Reverend, who's been here many more years than the rest of us, could explain

138

it. But I suppose some things are best left unspoken. Not here, at least."

"Well said," mumbled Doug, who must have understood less than a tenth of what Mr. Everett had told us up to that point.

"There were so many of them, as I said — and Wark wasn't even the angriest," Mr. Everett said.

"Wark?" I asked.

"Cumai's brother," Aiby guessed.

Mr. Everett nodded. "Precisely. All of them were furious. Even the big, stone ones. There was one Other in particular who kept talking angrily," he said. He rubbed his chin. "Which one was it? No, not the elemental . . . it looked like a woman. A stone woman, that's right! She was as sharp as a diamond and just as brilliant. So anyway, that was the situation when we arrived at the island. They were waiting for us, and they were furious."

We were all silent for a long time. I felt a sort of presence near us and turned to look at the apple tree in the cloister. It was covered by shadow, maybe from a cloud passing overhead.

"But if it hadn't been for that stone woman," Mr. Everett said, "perhaps they wouldn't have taken the Reverend hostage. If Prospero were with us now, perhaps we'd have a chance at finding out who killed Cumai . . ."

So that's why the Others were angry, I realized. *They knew that Cumai had been murdered and were insisting that the residents of Applecross hand the culprit over to them. They were holding the Reverend hostage until the killer was turned over to them!*

"But we know who it was!" Doug exclaimed. "Isn't that right, Viper?"

"Shut up, Doug!" I said, but it was too late.

Mr. Everett looked at him. "What did you say?"

"They told me who it was!" Doug said, pointing at Aiby and me.

"Is that true?" asked Mr. Everett.

A small thud came from the cloister behind us as a green apple fell from the tree. It rolled around in the flowers below.

"Who killed Cumai?" Mr. Everett insisted. "Tell me. Now."

"Askell," Aiby murmured.

"Semueld Askell?" Mr. Everett asked.

"Semueld Askell," I repeated.

Mr. Everett grabbed his head with his hands and tugged like he wanted to pull out his hair. "Oh, no, no, no! It's impossible, absolutely impossible!"

"Mr. Everett," said Aiby, "you two were friends, weren't you?"

"I heard you talking to Askell in your store," I added.

"It's true!" Mr. Everett said. "He has come in and spoken to me many times, certainly. He's a good guy . . . a good man! He just finished his studies at an excellent university. An economics degree from the University of Chicago, in fact. And he knows a lot about magic. He's asked me many questions and looked for lots of souvenirs. But it couldn't have been him."

"We found a shard from his cloak," I said.

"What cloak?" Mr. Everett asked.

"The one he wears to disguise himself and change shapes," Aiby whispered. "The Cloak of Mirrors."

Mr. Everett got to his feet then and leaned on his walking stick with both his hands. "Are you sure we're talking about the same person? The Semueld Askell I know is a pleasant young man who doesn't wear a cloak. I see him go jogging every morning along the coast, always between five and six in the morning. He's also a trekking enthusiast. He's asked for practically every map of the paths around the bay. To the best of my knowledge, he's staying here for a year here to write a book for his university."

"Do you know where he lives?" I asked.

"Yes, of course," Mr. Everett said. "At the campground."

Chapter
FIFTEEN

TENTS,
HIDEOUTS, &
TRAPS

The Applecross campground was just outside the village in the fields that surrounded the river. For a good part of the year, the Applecross River was little more than a harmless trickle. During the summer, when the first campers' tents started to appear, it swelled with water.

Hidden from both the coastal road and the one that climbed into the mountains, the campground housed most of the town's tourists. Bicyclists, kayakers, and trekkers all lodged there. Few of them arrived in cars since the mountain road was dangerous for inexperienced drivers. And besides, the coastal road was much more scenic.

Tourists stayed for a week at most, setting up

revolting barbecues on the lawn, or descending on the village to guzzle beers at the Greenlock Pub. Our tourists seemed to love sporting the worst possible combinations of socks and shorts.

McStay, who owned the inn, did not view them highly and therefore his pub didn't serve them the best mussels and shrimp. But the tourists always seemed happy anyway.

Strangely enough, if the weather grew cold and the campground was hit with a downpour, most tourists seemed even more satisfied with their vacations. Maybe they felt they got the authentic Scottish experience that way. Who knows.

All this, at least, is what Mr. Everett told us about them on the way from Cumai's mill to the entrance to the campground. But the second part of his story was much more interesting than his snobbish attitude toward the campers. He told us about his friendship with Cumai, with whom he said he'd spent years trading tales.

Previous to their companionship, Mr. Everett had often felt like a boring academic. He was pleasantly surprised by the interest Cumai showed in his field of research: art history.

In turn, Mr. Everett had been fascinated by the fantastic tales told by the strange lady of the mill. When

Aiby asked him what kind of tales these were, he told us one about a big tree with white leaves that suddenly sprouted a strange blue leaf.

It was a short and touching tale. Aiby was sniffling, so Mr. Everett handed her his handkerchief. Aiby thanked him for this odd act of gallantry and wiped her eyes, then slipped the handkerchief into my backpack. Patches marked his passage on the hedge that surrounded the campground, then he trotted inside and barked to announce his arrival to us.

The sky was becoming ominously dark. I checked the time on the watch that was ticking away softly in my jeans pocket. Aiby smiled at me, apparently glad I still had it with me.

There were about a dozen tents, each one set up a bit away from the others. A few wooden huts used for showers and toilets were located in the middle. Two cyclists were in the process of hanging a battalion of colored socks on a laundry line. Another two were perched on folding beach chairs while reading books on their tablets.

Even without Mr. Everett's guidance, we would've had no trouble guessing which tent was Semueld Askell's. At the far end of the campground was a round tent with a conical roof. Its walls were covered with hides and

145

furs. It looked like a small circus tent, except that it was completely white.

Behind the bizarre home, I noticed a giant black jeep with tinted windows and a roof antenna. I pointed it out to Doug.

"Now *that* is a jeep," he said in admiration.

We walked over to the tent without saying a word. It smelled of goat and other scents I couldn't quite place, though none of them were pleasant. Its only entrance was covered by a large, cracked leather hide.

"Semueld?" Mr. Everett called out loudly, stopping at the threshold. "Are you home?"

We waited a moment. Mr. Everett repeated his question. He finally turned to us. "Apparently he's not here," he said.

The hide covering the entrance to the tent rose slightly, as if inviting us to enter anyway.

"I don't think that's a good idea," I said.

Aiby slipped on the colored glasses and chose the violet lenses. After a quick look she said, "There isn't any protection magic present. It's just a tent."

"But it's still Semueld Askell's tent," I muttered. "And we certainly can't tell him we just happened to be passing through."

Aiby took off the glasses and nodded. "But this could

146

be our only opportunity to . . . take a quick look around. Then we can leave."

"Do you really think he'd let us? Don't you think it's strange he left all his things here without any sort of protection?" I said.

"The Fludd Lenses don't lie," Aiby said. "We have nothing to fear."

Mr. Everett looked inside somewhat uncomfortably. The two tablet readers had turned their backs to us and the sock hangers had disappeared having finished hanging their laundry.

"If you stand guard outside," Aiby said, "I'll go in and take a look."

I nodded. "Fine by me," I said.

"I'm coming with you, Aiby," Doug said.

"Why?" I protested.

"This isn't a good idea, kids," Mr. Everett said, but he said it like he meant the opposite. I got the feeling he'd brought us here precisely so we'd enter that tent.

"I'm not going inside," I said, watching for Mr. Everett's reaction.

"We'll only take a second," Aiby said, motioning for Doug to follow her inside.

I kept staring at Mr. Everett, wondering what game he was playing, and whose side he was on.

147

Aiby slipped beneath the leather hide that was protecting the entrance and inspected the interior. I said nothing, but I was pretty certain we were making the umpteenth mistake of the day. Doug followed her and let the hide drop to the ground behind them.

"Straight into the wolves' den," I whispered.

While we were waiting for Aiby and my brother to finish their reconnaissance, I asked Mr. Everett which island they'd taken old lady Cumai to. Mr. Everett's response was vague, claiming he hadn't been at the helm, it was the dead of night, and only Reverend Prospero knew the route.

"Was there a bonfire on that island?" I asked him.

"Yes," Mr. Everett said.

The Professor kept looking back and forth at the tent and the campgrounds as if he were waiting for something to happen.

It seemed like hours passed, though it had only been about five minutes. "How long have they been inside?" I asked.

"They should've come out by now," Mr. Everett said.

Patches wagged his tail as two cyclists appeared at the campground, towing their luggage in a bike cart behind them.

"He'll be back soon," Mr. Everett said, his tone grim. "We have to warn them."

"What do you intend to do?" I asked.

"Wait for me here," he said.

He lifted the hide and disappeared inside the tent.

I heard him calling out Doug and Aiby's names. "Let's get out of here!" he added.

There was no response. "Now what?" I said to myself.

I stood in front of Askell's giant, smelly tent, wondering why my three companions in adventure had gone silent. I considered taking out the silver watch I had in my pocket, just in case. Maybe I could pull the hand back one hour earlier so I could convince them not to enter the campground. I decided against it, since it didn't feel like the right time to use it.

Then I heard a child's laughter. The two cyclists who had just arrived had clearly not brought their luggage in the bike cart. Instead, a happy two-year-old boy poked his head out from the trailer.

Watching them, I found myself smiling and wishing I had traveled with my parents. My mom and dad hadn't been beyond Glasgow since my brother and I were born. Before that, they'd only been to London a few times.

Hearing the laughter, I put the watch back in my

pocket. If that little boy was happy, then it wasn't the right moment to turn back time. Besides, I figured everything was fine and I just needed to calm down.

"Maybe we should go inside," I whispered to my companion. "What do you think, Patches?"

As always, he agreed with me. So we went inside.

The interior of Askell's tent did not look at all like a tent, but rather a giant New York apartment. The floor was covered with white rugs and there were a few elegant lacquered trunks atop them. Between them were some gilded cushions scattered around.

In the middle of the tent was a massive black table cluttered with maps and instruments. On one side, a big hearth contained a roaring inferno worthy of a rocket ship. To the left of the entrance was a discarded machine that looked like an enormous dismantled washing machine, or maybe a turbine for a submarine.

The walls inside the tent were decorated with leopard skins, a large mirror, and an ultra-slim flat screen TV. On the opposite side, there was a huge feather mattress resting on the ground. The air was saturated with an exotic perfume — and a soft melody.

I took a few steps toward the table and noticed it was overflowing with compasses, bottles of different colors of ink, protractors, and rulers of various lengths.

Most interestingly, there were several maps of the Applecross peninsula, village, and bay. There were maps of the paths, nautical charts of the sea around the islands, topographical maps, title searches, and building interiors. I recognized the stamp from Mr. Everett's Curious Traveler on some of them. Others, however, were so old that they looked as if they'd come from a museum. Still others were so battered and stained that they would have looked right at home in a treasure chest at the bottom of the sea.

Some maps were hanging from rows of colored pins along the edges of the table. One in particular struck me: it was a complete map of England, but instead of listing the names of all the places, it displayed only a few that were identified with large, elaborate circles. To the side, there was some text written in the Enchanted Language.

I struggled to read the magical letters as they moved and shifted before my eyes. Eventually, I was able to make out the phrase: *Map of the Passages.*

Passages? I thought. *What kind of passages?*

I scanned the map and identified Scotland, then Applecross Bay. One of those strange circles was marking a remote islet. "Fladda-chùain," I read aloud in a whisper.

A slight chill ran down my spine as I realized I wasn't alone.

Chapter
SIXTEEN

SEMUELD,
FINLEY, &
AIBY

I turned around quickly and saw a shape in the shadows. "Aiby, is that you?" I murmured. "Doug? Mr. Everett?"

What had initially looked like the profile of a person turned out to be two stacks of books with grotesque African masks resting atop them. I was alone after all.

I let out a sigh and ventured a couple of steps closer to the table, wondering if I should take the map. My eyes were drawn to three items abandoned nearby in the center of a rug. As I stepped closer, I identified a violin, a colored scarf, and a wand.

I recognized the scarf right away, which sent another shiver down my spine.

I kneeled down next to Patches. "Do you recognize it, boy?" I asked. "It's the scarf Cumai always wore!"

Patches moved closer to sniff it, but jerked to a halt when an icy voice murmured, "Well said, young McPhee. All three of those items were hers. An authentic Sidhe Violin, a Good Times Scarf, and a Berry Questing Wand."

Semueld Askell appeared out of thin ar near the four-post bed. He was a tall man with a long, thin nose that gave him a sly appearance. His shiny hair was neatly combed back, and he was dressed in black from head to toe. His hands were unfastening the Cloak of Mirrors that had undoubtedly kept him hidden until that point.

"But they're worthless items," he continued. "Little more than odds and ends, really. I'd hoped they'd be able to help me in some way, but no."

Askell untied the cloak completely and threw it onto the bed in irritation. He slowly massaged his temples and said with a grimace, "I've been waiting for you, McPhee. I was beginning to wonder how long it would take you to find me. Last night, your brother interrupted me before I could finish writing my invitation. I'm glad you found my home despite that fact."

I clenched my teeth and nudged Patches closer to me with my toe. "Where are my friends?" I snarled.

Askell stepped closer. "Ah, yes," he said. "Those were your friends? All of them?"

I didn't respond. Everything Semueld asked seemed like it had a deeper, sinister meaning.

Askell glanced at the three magical objects that had belonged to Cumai, then sighed theatrically. "I must say that young Lily's naiveté really surprised me. Perhaps her father never taught her the first rule of magical objects?"

"And what would that be?" I said petulantly.

Semueld took a step closer and tilted his head at me. "If they're not yours, then don't touch them," he said. He pulled a pair of green gloves out of his pocket and slowly put them on.

"What did you do to them?" I said through clenched teeth.

"I did nothing to them. They did it to themselves." He leaned over to pick up the violin. "Cumai's magical objects had their own antitheft system, shall we say. And your *friends* tried to take them without permission." I frowned, puzzled. Was it possible that Aiby's magical glasses didn't reveal those perils?

Semueld Askell spun the violin between his fingers. "Do you know how to play, McPhee? I don't, and that's perhaps the one regret I have. Every so often I tell myself I should learn, but in fact I never do. I would love to play

155

the piano. To practice arpeggios, scales . . . anything, really."

He set the violin on the table and stared at a random spot on the ceiling of the tent. Softly, slowly, he began to sing, "Don't ask me again: what answer can I give you? I don't like haggard cheeks and dimming eyes. Yet, my friend, I don't want you to die. Don't ask me again. Your destiny and mine are sealed." Then he looked at me and asked, "Do you know that song?"

"No," I admitted. Still, it felt like I'd heard the melody before. Maybe at school? Or in a movie?

"It doesn't matter," Semueld said. "Forget about it. We aren't here to talk about music, right?"

"I don't think so," I said softly. Patches growled.

"Well then, let's talk about what we should be talking about," Semueld said.

"Tell me what happened to Aiby and my brother," I demanded.

Askell chuckled.

I frowned. "Look, we know that you —"

Askell cut me off by raising both hands as if to protect his face. "We're starting poorly, McPhee, very poorly. Accusing me of crimes in my own home is outside the bounds of hospitality. Let's instead discuss this like magicians. Or, if you prefer, like gentlemen. After all,

until the last century, the terms were synonymous with each other."

"Gentlemen don't kill," I said.

Askell laughed heartily. "A youthful perspective, McPhee, and let's hope you can keep thinking that for a long time! I'm sorry to contradict you, but not only do gentlemen kill, they often happen to do so without reason. Just for fun."

"What about you? Why do you do it?" I asked.

He sneered. "I think you know."

"Maybe," I said, baiting him. "But I'd rather you tell me yourself."

"As you wish," Semueld said. "I'm searching for something that an ancestor of your friend Aiby stole many years ago. An item that none of the Lilys wants to give to me."

"What did they steal from you?" I asked.

"Oh, they didn't steal it from me. They stole it from *everyone*."

"Everyone?" I asked.

"From *everyone*," Semueld Askell repeated. "And I believe the time has come for them to return it."

"How can someone steal something that belongs to everyone?" I asked.

Semueld Askell chewed one of his fingernails. "Too

157

many questions, young McPhee. You ask too many questions."

"Aiby says that Reginald Lily didn't steal anything," I said.

"Oh, really? What a coincidence! You even know the name of the thief! I never said Reginald Lily stole what I'm looking for at all! The man with the red wooden ship that was wrecked near here also happens to be hated by the giants . . . don't you find that to be a very strange coincidence?"

"Aiby says that —" I began.

"Cut it out, McPhee!" Askell interrupted. "'She says this, she says that!' Is Aiby here right now? Do you hear someone talking other than me? I don't — besides the annoying chirp of a weak little boy who I've heard is supposed to be none other than the Enchanted Emporium's defender."

I flared up with rage and shivered with fear. The skin on my neck prickled and I slipped my hands into my pocket. As soon as my fingers touched the scorpion key, Askell began speaking again. "I'm going to give you just one piece of advice, McPhee. Don't try to use any magical object that you brought with you, because it won't work inside my tent. And before you ask, I'll tell

158

you why: we're in the yurt of Temujin, the lord of the Golden Horde. Did you ever study his exploits with the Mongolian army?"

I shook my head. It made no difference to me whether Temujin was a real historical figure or the main character in a fantasy novel.

"I believe Mr. Lily can explain to you in detail how this tent works," Askell continued. "And perhaps you can read in the *BBMO* that a very powerful Silence of the Voices is in effect in here, which cancels out any unwelcome magic. But I don't think you're all that interested in the art of magic, right?"

I said nothing because he was right. And in any case, I understood the essence of the information perfectly: no magical objects worked here. That, at least, explained why Aiby's glasses had not helped her.

"Do you like it?" Askell asked me, waving his arms around with an expansive gesture.

"It stinks like a goat," I said.

He laughed. "Very true! An authentic goat stink from Mongolia! But this tent is a portable gem, which my family got ahold of under very singular circumstances," Askell explained.

In that moment, Askell reminded me of a vulture

circling above a carcass, waiting for the right moment to descend.

"What do you want from me?" I asked, trying to appear calmer than I actually was. Patches yelped when I accidentally stepped on his tail.

"You really have no idea?" Askell asked.

"No."

"I think you do. And I'd like you to figure it out yourself," Askell replied. "You know that I'm looking for something, and that I've looked through all the houses, ruined castles, and wrecks on the peninsula." He picked up a couple of maps and let them drop back onto the table. "Every house, with the exception of one. A very special house that I cannot enter."

"So why can't you enter the Enchanted Emporium?" I asked.

"Because I'm one of the seven shopkeepers, my young friend. And we aren't allowed to enter while another family is running the shop."

"That's not my problem," I said.

Askell smiled. "Too true. It's entirely mine. And it's also the reason why I've been waiting for you with such trepidation. Look, the only way I can enter the Enchanted Emporium and take back what I've been looking for is if you give me your key."

I clutched the scorpion key in my hand, thinking back to the previous evening when the ravens had ransacked my box of precious possessions without finding the key hidden in the false bottom.

"You could have just taken it last night," I reminded him.

Askell snickered. "Oh, that would've been too easy. I mean, yes, I could have taken it from that ridiculous false bottom of your box of trifling things, but it wouldn't have been the same. The shopkeepers have been carefully protected from the risk of accidentally losing one of the keys. When the families established the rules of succession for the Emporiums, they did things right: they found four special keys, which the shopkeepers called *Archetypes*. Otherwise known as objects created before the First Magical Revolution. These keys are four of the most powerful magical objects around."

Askell took a few steps closer to me. "Look, McPhee, the truth is that I can't just *take* your key. You have to give it to me — of your own free will. I know it may seem absurd to you, but that's how it works." Askell coughed nervously. "In other words, I need . . . well, I need your permission."

"And why should I give it to you?" I said.

"Because I know what you'd like in exchange."

"Oh? So you know me know?" I challenged.

"With certainty."

Semueld Askell came even closer. My goosebumps got goose bumps. Patches bared his teeth. A deafening silence spread over the tent.

"You want the heart of that girl," Semueld Askell whispered. Slowly, he bent his neck and leaned over me like a bird of prey. "You want to capture the heart of Aiby Lily."

CLOAK OF MIRRORS

AMONG THE MANY CLOAKS OF
INVISIBILITY THAT APPEAR IN FAIRY
TALES, THIS IS UNDOUBTEDLY THE
MOST POWERFUL ONE. ORIGINATING
IN ANCIENT IRAN, THE CLOAK ONCE
BELONGED TO THE OLD MAN OF THE
MOUNTAIN. EXTREMELY LIGHT BUT
STRONG AS IRON ARMOR, THE CLOAK
ALLOWS ITS WEARER TO BLEND IN
WITH THEIR SURROUNDINGS. THE
WEARER CAN ALSO APPEAR AS A
GROUP OF RAVENS, MICE, SQUIRRELS,
SNAKES, FROGS, OR CATFISH.

ENCHANTED EMPORIUM

Chapter
SEVENTEEN

BOXES,
TRUNKS, &
CASKETS

Time stopped in Temujin's yurt. Or at least it seemed to stop. After inspecting me with his frosty eyes, Askell withdrew a few steps.

"I'd say I guessed correctly, McPhee," he said.

I couldn't speak. He was right again, after all. Ever since I'd first laid eyes on Aiby Lily in the village, nothing interested me more. When I had faced giants, solved riddles in bottles, chased dangerous thieves who had stolen magic books, bet my soul in a game of cards, and risked my life plunging from the tower into the bay, I had always been thinking of her. There were plenty of reasons to do the things I'd done, but Aiby had always been *my* reason.

"Cat got your tongue, McPhee?" Semueld Askell said, turning his back to me.

If only I could've taken advantage of that moment to flee with Patches, or if I'd had one of Askell's darts from his blowgun. Perhaps then things would have gone differently. Then again, maybe I never would've even reached the end of that summer.

I remained silent, so he continued. "If you'd prefer, you can just nod. You want to capture the heart of that girl, right?"

I nodded.

"And you want it now."

I nodded my head a second time.

Askell extended a hand protected by a green glove and grabbed a small box from the table. "Then here, take it!" he exclaimed. "Now her heart is yours!"

With one fluid motion, he threw the box to me. Patches barked and I, stupidly, did the one thing I shouldn't have done: I caught it.

"Ouch!" I cried out. "It bit me!"

That couldn't have been possible, but that's what it felt like. The small box was decorated with shells and colored inlays in a tribal pattern. On the lid, the lock was shaped like the head of an ebony monkey, its keyhole designed to accept something shaped like a shark's tooth.

It was slightly open. And it was empty.

I was tempted to drop it to the ground because of its frightening appearance, but I forced myself to keep it balanced on the palm of my hand. It was a little bigger than Aiby's glasses, and it smelled like something between nutmeg and sulfur.

"All you have to do is place four things from your beloved into the Heart-eating Box," Askell said. "Something from the body, something from the dead, something that's liquid, and something worn."

I looked at it, appalled by its name. Askell began counting out loud on his fingers. "Something from the body can be a lock of hair or a fingernail. Something from the dead must have belonged to one of her ancestors, preferably one of her parents. For something that's liquid, a tear or some of her saliva. And I don't think I need to explain the last one. Find these four things, put them in the box, close the lock, and Aiby Lily's heart will be yours forever."

"And if I don't close it?" I asked.

"It depends," Semueld Askell responded. "Is the box open or closed right now?"

"Open," I said.

"That's a real pity!" Askell declared. "Once it's open, you only have the length of one day to put the things

you need inside it. Give me your key to the Enchanted Emporium and in exchange you'll get Aiby Lily's heart. Of course, you can decide not to give me the key, and then . . ."

"Then what?" I asked.

Askell shrugged. "The box will eat you," he said.

I stared at the grinning monkey on the lock. "But I don't want this . . . thing," I said. At that moment, I thought about the words Askell had written on the wall in my room about playing a game.

"But you took the box," Askell said. "And you opened it, as well."

"I didn't open it!" I shouted. "It opened all on its own!"

I threw the box into the middle of the tent. It landed on the rugs with a soft thump. What happened next still makes my skin crawl: the box crawled back to me, walking on the floor with two rows of fiendish little legs. Patches barked fiercely as it approached, but the Heart-eating Box didn't stop moving until it touched the tip of my toe.

Semueld Askell smirked. "Once you've let them out, you can't play with feelings, McPhee," he said. "Especially when they're strong ones, like your feelings for that silly girl."

I kicked the box away, but it just righted itself and started marching toward me again. "Get it away from me!" I screamed.

"I'm sorry, young McPhee," Semueld said. "There's nothing you nor I can do about it now."

Patches barked even louder and scratched the Heart-eating Box with one of his paws. He crouched low and kept biting the box as if it were an insect.

"The box will follow you everywhere, just like your ridiculous, furry friend," Semueld said. He clapped his hands. In response, one of the black trunks that were scattered around the tent opened wide and jumped at Patches.

"No!" I shrieked. I watched helplessly as my dog disappeared into the trunk. It snapped shut with a dull thud. "Patches!"

I went over to the trunk and gave it a savage kick, but all I got was a yelp from my poor dog.

"Finally a bit of peace and quiet," Askell remarked.

"Let him go right now!" I shouted.

"Do you know how those work?" Semueld asked. "This is a Strange Sarcophagi based on the model of the original Egyptian ones. The name comes from the Greek words *sarx* and *phagein*, which mean *meat* and *eat*, respectively." Semueld smirked. "I prefer the Strange

Sarcophagi to traditional coffins for a variety of personal reasons."

"Shut up!" I screamed. "Just stop your incessant blabbering and give me back my dog RIGHT THIS MINUTE!"

"So you don't want the others back, too?" Semueld asked, jingling a set of four small keys in his hand. He pointed to the other trunks scattered around the tent. That's when I realized where Aiby, Doug, and Mr. Everett had gone.

"It's up to you, young McPhee," Semueld continued. "It's all up to you. I believe I've been rather generous, all things considered. I've given you the box so you can win Aiby Lily's heart, and you have until tomorrow night to decide whether to give me the key to the Enchanted Emporium or get eaten by the box."

Semueld began singing a song similar to the melancholy tune from before: "In a way, it's mad; in a way, it's sad; what I need for satisfaction, I can't get through my own action . . ."

"Stop it!" I shouted.

"You have one day to think things over, Finley McPhee. You can have everything, or nothing." He laughed. "When you've decided what to do . . . call me!"

With that said, he retrieved the Cloak of Mirrors and donned it. Before I could do or say anything, the interior of the tent dissipated into a flock of fleeing ravens.

Blowgun of Aesculapius

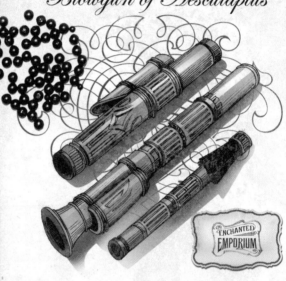

Carved from a long hollow shaft of elderwood, the Blowgun of Aesculapius is a Sidhe's favorite weapon for causing mayhem. They are capable of shooting little clay balls (headache pebbles), darts (Sidhe Strikes) and heart arrows (honey-soaked arrows that cause their targets to weaken and fall in love). When used by magical creatures, the blowgun shoots metal projectiles (iron, gold, or silver).

MISTAKES, CIRCUMSTANCES, & OPPORTUNITIES

I dodged past black wings and beaks, then fell to the ground shouting. The flock of ravens dispersed into the sky and vanished against the sunset.

I picked myself up and looked around. The two campers who were reading didn't seem to have noticed anything that had happened. Neither had the two cyclists with the carriage.

I ran over to the bicycle attached to the trailer and hopped on. "I'll bring it back as soon as possible!" I shouted at them, pedaling away. "Sorry, but it's an emergency!"

Despite their objections, I raced toward the village with all my might. I felt the weight of the cart behind

me, but I didn't stop pedaling even though I wasn't sure where I was going.

I saw the flock of ravens flying high in the sky and deluded myself into thinking that I could somehow follow them to find out where Askell was headed. Once on the coastal road, I saw that the ravens were heading inland on the peninsula, over the mountains.

What is in the mountains? I thought. *There's the pass, there's the dam . . . the dam!*

I was sure they were going to the dam! But why, exactly? What was Semueld Askell going to do all the way up there?

I didn't know, nor did I know why the two tourists whose bike I'd stolen were still screaming at me. I turned to see the man was running after me like a madman. *Is his bike one of those ultra-light and super expensive ones?* I wondered. *Didn't he hear me say I'll return it?*

"Wah," whimpered the little boy in the cart behind me. "Wah."

I slammed on the brakes. I was a perfect idiot. I took one last look at the ravens that were flying away, now impossible to catch up to, and climbed off the bike.

"I'm so sorry!" I said to the little boy, not really knowing what else to do. He stared at me with his large, curious eyes and smiled. He must have enjoyed being

carted around as I'd pedaled. His father, on the other hand, looked anything but pleased. If he caught me, he would throttle me. And he would be right to do so.

The dad had almost reached me. With horror, I saw the Heart-eating Box scurrying behind him. My stomach tied in knots, I took off in a dash toward the village, running as fast as I possibly could.

What should I do? I asked myself, unable to think anything but those words. The ravens had disappeared. Aiby was trapped in a trunk, and so were my brother, Mr. Everett, and Patches. Askell had the keys to the trunks and would only give them to me in exchange for the key to the Enchanted Emporium.

"Never!" I snarled, continuing to run.

Then there was the Heart-eating Box, which within twenty-four hours would either deliver Aiby's heart to me . . . or eat me.

Maybe I should have returned to the campground and tried to open the trunks. Maybe I should have run to the Enchanted Emporium to ask Mr. Lily for help. I could have run home, hoping that the box wouldn't catch me, and then explain everything to Dad. "Listen, Dad! Doug, my girlfriend, and Mr. Everett are trapped in magical trunks, along with Patches. And the person who did it is Semueld Askell, an economist from Chicago who deals

in magical objects and is staying at the campground in a magical tent. And you also should know, Dad, that this Askell is the same person who killed old lady Cumai, and that Cumai's brother is ready to lead an uprising of magical beings against Applecross unless we deliver the culprit. But first, they'll probably kill Reverend Prospero."

Knowing my father, he would have interrupted me before I'd managed to get halfway through that speech, and then he would've sent me to my room without dinner.

Unfortunately, going to Somerled was out of the question since Scary Villa was too far away.

What about Meb? I thought. *It's evening, so she might still be at her shop.*

"Please, please, please," I said, running through the country roads like a maniac. "Please still be at work, Meb . . ."

But Meb wasn't there. The note on the door of her store read: *CLOSED.*

No Meb, no Reverend Prospero, no Dad. I considered running to Reginald Bay to Mr. Lily, but I had no form of transportation. I briefly considered lying down and going fetal, hoping for the best.

The sun had set, and the sky was tinged with violet. I tried to think and breathe. I felt smothered by the little time I had left to figure out what to do. I slipped off the backpack and dug inside it.

"Maybe there's something I can use in here," I said to myself.

I pulled out Aiby's spare T-shirt, Mr. Everett's handkerchief, a metal water bottle, and two Essential Pouches containing the shard from the cloak and the arrowhead. There was a pack of flowery tissues with words in the Enchanted Language written on the package, a pocket knife that looked anything but magical, and the case for the Fludd Lenses.

"No magic ticket for quickly getting back home," I said, failing to read the instructions in the Enchanted Language on the wrapper. "Come on, there has to be something useful in here . . ."

I heard a clicking sound behind me and remembered the box was still chasing me. I shoved everything back into the backpack and headed toward the pub. Maybe someone there would be willing to give me a ride to Reginald Bay.

I ran down the only alley in all of Applecross and headed toward the square. I heard shouting in the street

ahead of me and ran as fast as I could toward the Curious Traveler.

My jaw dropped. "No!" I cried out. "It can't be. It simply can't be!"

In the middle of the road, between the shop and the Greenlock Pub, was one of Askell's trunks. It was standing vertically. A crowd had formed around it.

Even at that distance, I could hear Mr. Everett's far-off voice and the furious pounding coming from inside the sarcophagus. Making my way through the crowd, I noticed a large mailing label that'd been glued to the side of the trunk. It read:

FRAGILE! THIS SIDE UP.

For delivery to the Curious Traveler

Applecross Square (Scotland)

Handle with care — contains Mr. Edwin Everett

To be opened preferably before midnight

To open, ask Mr. Finley McPhee of Applecross (Scotland)

"What a coward," I cried after reading the last lines.

Mr. McStay grabbed me by the collar. "What happened to Edwin, kid?"

I ignored him. Leaning on the trunk, I said, "Mr. Everett, it's Finley! Don't worry, I'll get you out of there!"

An eerie wailing came from inside the trunk that made my skin crawl. I dashed away, steering clear of the panicked crowd.

What have I done? I wondered.

Soon I'd reached the coastal road. I crossed it and leaped onto the stony beach, running until I felt water squish inside my shoes. I collapsed in a heap, unable to think or move. I was completely alone and panicked. Night was falling like ink pooling on an empty page.

If Mr. Everett was delivered in front of his store, Doug should have also been delivered to the farm. Perhaps the headlights I saw flashing south of the village toward my house were from my father's van as he left to look for me.

And Aiby? Aiby might have been delivered to the Enchanted Emporium. That would be a good thing since it'd mean Mr. Lily and Meb would know about the danger. But they wouldn't yet know what we'd discovered at the mill, nor about the island where Reverend Prospero was being held prisoner. Or about Cumai's brother.

I felt like I'd lost my mind. I was already hearing all the questions they would ask me.

Why did you go to the mill without telling us, Finley?

Why did you enter Askell's tent, Finley?

Finley, why is your brother trapped in a trunk?

What did you do this time, Finley?

Finley, aren't you supposed to be the defender of the Enchanted Emporium?

"No!" I screamed, panicked by anger and guilt. I got back on my feet, grabbed a rock, and squeezed it between my fingers until they hurt. "I never wanted to become the Enchanted Emporium's defender! I don't care at all about magical objects. I just wanted to fish quietly at the pond!"

I hurled the rock into the sea.

"It's Aiby's fault! It's all Aiby's fault!" I repeated. "If it hadn't been for her — if she hadn't . . ."

I didn't even understand what was making me angry. Hot, guilty tears flowed down my cheeks. I wiped them away with the back of my hand. Only a few hours before, Aiby too had wiped away her tears with Mr. Everett's handkerchief.

"This sucks," I said.

Clickety-clack.

Clickety-clickety-clack.

I turned and saw the Heart-eating Box scuttling along the stone beach with determined zeal. I saw the

striped shells on its sides that looked like so many tiny mouths.

It caught up with me, brushed against my foot in the sand, and stopped. I picked it up. "Everything's gone wrong," I said to it. "Everything's all wrong."

Several cars arrived in the village. I heard distant voices. Some of the villagers were calling for Mr. McStay. I clearly heard the Reverend's name mentioned.

The sky grew darker still, like a curtain being drawn before the stars took the stage. I wanted to dissolve. Disappear. To erase my birth from the history of Applecross.

I gazed at the empty interior of the box, thinking it would be just big enough to put the four small items inside. I thought that even if I gave my key to Askell and the Emporium closed, at least I would still have Aiby. The Heart-eating Box would link the two of us together forever, which was a magnificent and terrible thought.

Everything was in my hands. I could choose to do nothing and let myself get eaten by that box, or I could offer up Aiby's heart instead. I could hold onto the key as the Enchanted Emporium's defender and try every possible means — magical or otherwise — to open the sarcophagi that Doug, Aiby, Patches, and Mr. Everett had been trapped in.

Then, without even thinking, I slipped Everett's handkerchief — still wet with Aiby's tears — into the box. Then I stuffed her shirt into it. It didn't take much time to find a few of her long hairs inside the backpack — she left them everywhere, like a mark of her passing. I held one of her hairs before my eyes, examining it in the little light that remained. It reminded me of a question mark.

I placed it inside the box, too.

Something from the body, something that's liquid, and something that is worn were all inside the box now. I was only missing the last item: something from the dead. I needed something that had belonged to one of her ancestors. And I had that, too. I took the Second Chance Watch and, watching it shine in the darkness, thought back to Aiby's words when she had given it to me. As if she had already foreseen everything that would happen.

Is that why you insisted on going into Askell's tent? I asked Aiby in my thoughts.

I was about to place the Watch inside the box when I heard someone call out. "Finley! Finley, are you there?"

In the distance, I recognized Dad's voice as well as Meb's. They had seen the trunks and were looking for me, unaware that I was very near them, shielded only by the shadow of the boats beached by the fishermen.

182

My name, as spoken by my father, echoed in my ears along with each new wave from the sea. I looked inside the open box at Aiby's hair, her shirt, the handkerchief with her tears, and the Second Chance Watch that was ticking in my hand.

Aiby had told me that if something irreparable should happen, I could try to move the single hand of the watch backward and have a second chance. Just once. Once in a lifetime.

I had already made so many mistakes. I couldn't afford to make any more of them. I had to figure this out. I had to do the right thing. For Aiby. For Doug and Patches, too.

"How far back do I need to go?" I asked the Watch, as if it would answer me. "And what will happen to everyone else? And to everything I have with me? Will it all disappear, too? Will this box disappear along with it?"

The monkey's head on the box was watching me. It seemed to be whispering something, its mouth moving ever so slightly. I brought the box closer to my face.

"What?" I whispered.

I couldn't hear it say anything, but up close it looked like the monkey's head was saying, "Six inches and six months. Six inches and six months." Clearly, I was losing my mind. That, or the box was a mind-reading jerk.

Neither option boded well for me.

"Aiby," I murmured, "how does this watch work? Why are there so many things I should know, but don't?"

I felt the water squishing between my toes in my shoes. From the sounds of the voices nearby, it seemed as if everyone was gathered in front of the pub around Mr. Everett's trunk. They sounded angry. And they kept saying my name . . .

I heard a sound in the air above me and looked up to see the ravens departing from the mountains.

I was tired of thinking things over.

It was time to act.

"To hell with it!" I said. "I don't owe you anything, Askell!"

I furiously pulled back the single hand of the Second Chance Watch.

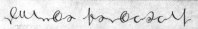

STRANGE
SARCOPHAGI

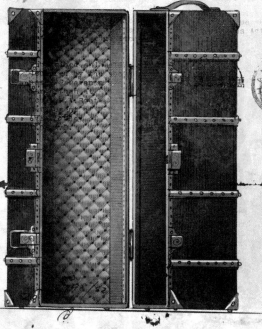

These coffins hail from the ancient Egyptian era. They were placed
at the entrances of the most important tombs to ward off
intruders and looters. The word *sarcophagus* means "eater of flesh,"
which perfectly illustrates how the Strange Sarcophagi work:
if someone approaches (in hopes of discovering treasure),
then the sarcophagus captures the intruder's
body and slowly devours it.

SECONDS, SECOND CHANCES, & A SECOND PLAN

The watch jumped out of my hands like a spring and struck the rocks on the beach. The glass cover shattered and the hand broke off the face. I picked it up, wondering if I'd done something wrong.

I looked around. The stars were still out. The sea was black and sleek just like before. The waves continued to lap at my shoes. The ravens that had come down from the mountains were now heading south. Toward my house.

Something bumped my foot. The Heart-eating Box was still there. The handkerchief, Aiby's hair, and her shirt were still inside.

The villagers hadn't moved from the front of the pub and Mr. Everett's shop. I saw the parked cars and heard

the same shouting as before. I shook my head, gripped by a profound weariness.

"Figures," I said to myself. "Nothing's ever that easy."

I felt naive to have believed that there could be a magical object powerful enough to let me turn back time. Instead of giving me a second chance it had fallen to pieces and now lay useless in my palm.

"I might as well toss it into the Heart-eating Box and forget about it," I said.

In the distance, I saw a few torches in a line leading down a path. At the top of the hill, the embers of a bonfire burned brightly.

My eyes went wide. I couldn't breathe. I put the watch in my pocket and the box into my backpack. I began running along the beach. I stumbled over the rocks until I reached the coastal road where the first group of men dressed in black were entering the pub. I opened the door and a ball of fur darted between the legs of the patrons and ran to meet me, barking all the while.

"Patches!" I cried out, unable to believe my eyes.

It's the previous night! I realized. *The night of Cumai's funeral!*

I bent down to pet Patches behind the ears, happier than ever. "It's amazing, Patches! It worked, little buddy! The Second Chance Watch really worked!"

I saw my brother. "Doug! Oh, Doug! I'm so happy!" I ran to him and hugged him, thrilled he was no longer trapped in a trunk. Doug just stood there with his arms at his sides, vaguely embarrassed.

"What's gotten into you, Viper?" he whispered, glancing back and forth. "And how did you change clothes so quickly?"

Doug was surprised because from his perspective he'd only lost sight of me for a few seconds. I let go of him, explaining that I'd brought a change of clothes in my backpack. He shrugged in response.

I tried to recall every detail about that point in the evening. By then, Aiby had already handed me the watch and had asked me to come see her at the Enchanted Emporium the next morning . . .

"Where's Aiby?" I asked Doug.

"Seriously?" Doug said. "We were just saying a few minutes ago that she and her father disappeared, tapping their heels! What's wrong with you, Viper?"

"Oh, right!" I said. "Of course!"

I quickly added up all the differences from the first time I'd been through that evening. I no longer had the working watch, but I did have the key to the Enchanted Emporium in my pocket. So the key wouldn't be under my bed where the ravens would look for it shortly.

I still had the Heart-eating Box, so Askell could no longer deliver it to me if I went back to his tent. Aiby's shirt was with me instead of at her house, and Mr. Everett no longer had the handkerchief he'd given to her. And the evidence we'd gathered at the mill was . . . where? I felt like my head was about to explode.

I walked through the pub just as I had the previous evening. The other villagers acted exactly as I remembered. Each of them was living through their own time, unaware of my second chance. I spoke again with Piper and Seamus about the stones around the fire. Then, just as it had occurred in the previous version of that evening, Reverend Prospero interrupted Seamus, who then pointed out that it was nearly midnight.

"Don't go, Reverend!" I cried out, realizing that the men were leaving for Cumai's burial at sea — and that Reverend Prospero would be taken hostage.

"I'm sorry, where shouldn't I go?" the Reverend asked me, surprised by my outburst.

That's a tricky question to answer, I realized.

I figured I could explain to him that I knew where he was headed, and that when he reached the island, he'd be taken hostage. Either he wouldn't believe me, or he'd continue on and do the same things. But if he believed me, everything would change. For both of us.

190

The one real advantage I had reliving this night was that I already knew what others would do, including Askell. Therefore, it was absolutely essential that everyone did the same things that they'd done the first time around. The less influence I had on their actions, the closer they'd stick to their original choice, and the more I'd be able to take advantage of my second chance.

I had to play a dangerous game without anyone becoming aware of my scheme. I'd have to challenge all of them: Askell, Aiby and Mr. Lily, Mr. Everett, and the Others on the island. Me against them all, Finley McPhee against the world. Did I even have a chance of succeeding?

I looked at Patches, my brother, and Mr. Everett. I imagined them trapped inside Askell's trunks again, and the answer came to me instantly: of course I could do it.

I smiled at Reverend Prospero and said, "I was just saying, Reverend, that it's a nice party and you should stay a little longer."

The Reverend frowned, grasped Seamus's shoulder, and led him away. I sighed with relief and tried to remember what I had done done next the evening before.

It was a strange sensation, being omniscient. I was watching people as if they weren't real — even though, underneath it all, this time was much more real than the

time before — because this was the only second chance in my lifetime. My last chance.

So I concentrated. I knew, for example, that a few minutes later I'd had a conversation with Somerled McBlack via the sapling in her father's van.

I approached Mr. Everett, who I knew was looking for his jacket. I asked him point-blank, "Excuse me, Mr. Everett, may I ask you a question? Do you remember that apple tree at Cumai's house?"

He seemed rather surprised to see me. "Yes. Why?" Then he realized what he'd just admitted and tried to backpedal. "I meant to say, what apple tree? There's no apple tree at Cumai's house."

I stared him straight in the eye and realized he *had* seen it. *So you're a Borderpasser, too,* I realized. *And I'd bet you took us to Askell's tent on purpose.*

I reminded myself to keep cool. I had to play things just like before. "Oh. I must be mistaken," I said, and then I left.

"Psst!" went the sapling in McBlack's van.

I didn't hesitate for a moment. "I'm here, Somerled!" I replied.

I was already planning my next moves at top speed. I figured Somerled would play a fundamental role in my second chance, especially because she was pretty much

the only person who could understand my situation besides Aiby. I han't intended to inform Aiby about my second chance, however.

"How did you know it was me?" the sapling asked.

"Somerled, I know that you're four hundred years old and that you came to Applecross with McBlack in search of a Passage that would let you return home. I know you want to tell me all this at the Black Birch, as well as the fact that Semueld Askell murdered Cumai with a Sidhe Strike. I know you want to give me the wooden key to the old mill. I know these things because I've already lived through this day once and I don't have time to explain why or how. So please listen to me carefully: unless I'm completely crazy, which is a definite possibility, I know which island the Passage to the Hollow World can be found on: Fladda-chùain. I saw it marked on a map called the Map of the Passages. I can take you there right now, this evening. I know your father will be gone the whole night to bury Cumai at sea, so there won't be any danger. Go to the Black Birch right now and from there go down the cliff path. Do it in a way that prevents the Lilys from noticing you. I'll be there waiting for you."

A gentle breeze blew through the sapling. "Okay," Somerled replied.

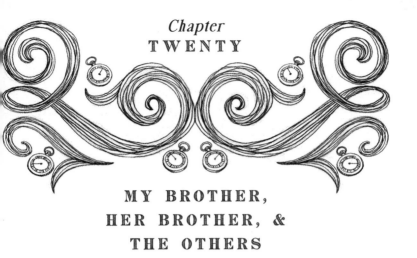

Chapter
TWENTY

MY BROTHER,
HER BROTHER, &
THE OTHERS

I had decided that I needed a helper in order to tackle the next part, and that helper would be Doug. While Somerled was the only person who could help me and understand what had happened in the course of delivering Cumai to the Others, Doug was the only one who could help me *without* necessarily understanding what was going on. Unfortunately for me, I knew that Doug's assistance would come with a price.

"Now listen up, Doug," I said, leading my brother back into the pub.

I spoke quickly but clearly, insisting that Doug convince my father and mother to go back home without us. I knew that Doug's boat was docked on the shore

since he was planning on using it to take Aiby on their picnic. I explained to him that the two of us absolutely had to use it to go out to sea that night, and it was essential that Doug drive the boat.

"I know it seems crazy," I concluded, "but if you agree to go out to sea with me tonight, I'll give you this." I showed him the key belonging to the Enchanted Emporium's defender.

Doug frowned. "What do I do with that?" he asked.

"Pay close attention, Doug. Only the true owner of one of the four keys to the Enchanted Emporium can decide to give theirs to someone else. And I've decided to give mine to you. Do you accept it?"

Doug took the scorpion key in his hand and glanced at it uncertainly. "That's all good and well," he said, "but the fact remains that I still don't understand what I can do with it."

"Doug, don't you get it?" I said. "You'll have the key to the Enchanted Emporium. You'll be its defender and . . . and you'll be Aiby's hero!"

Doug's eyes went wide. He looked at the key in an an entirely different way. "And Aiby told you to give the key to me?"

"Just so," I lied, pushing away the shame as best I

could. "You can have it, but you have to swear to me that you won't give it to anyone else — no matter what."

"Sure, sure," said Doug.

"Do you swear it?" I pushed.

"What?" he asked me.

"That you won't give that key to anyone, no matter the reason."

"Sure," Doug said again.

"Okay, you swore it," I said. "Now can we please go get the boat? Another one of my friends is waiting at the cliff."

I had the feeling that with this story of being Aiby's hero and the friend who was waiting for me at the cliff, Doug would think of me entirely differently now.

We reached Reginald Bay fifteen minutes later. The shadows were so dense that Doug didn't notice that Somerled's skin was a translucent olive color and her veins were golden brown.

Somerled hesitated before climbing in the boat. I whispered in her ear a few of the things she would tell me many hours later, which convinced her to follow me.

"Now let's go to Fladda-chùain," I said, revealing the second part of my plan. Doug protested, telling me that he didn't know where it was. After I told him, he

197

said that it was too far away. In response, I produced the pack of flowered tissues with the instructions in the Enchanted Language.

"Just read this," I said to my brother.

Doug squinted. "Windy Hankies," he read. "When waved by a sea voyager, they accelerate the owner's vessel across the water at high speed."

He looked at me. "High speed?" he repeated. "How high?"

I winked. "Let's find out."

I untied the flowered Hankies and began waving one with my hand while muttering an amusing farewell under my breath. The nose of the boat tilted up as if pushed by a sudden, fierce wind. A second later, the boat was zooming across the waves as if the outboard motor was nuclear powered.

Doug grinned and took a seat at the controls. "Keep waving, Viper!" he cried.

After waving a few more hankies, it felt like our boat was speeding along without even touching the waves. Doug laughed like a madman while Somerled crouched low in the bow of the boat and patiently listened to my tale of the day I'd already experienced.

An hour passed like this. Eventually, Somerled

agreed to put on a performance that would match how she'd acted the previous day. It seemed she thought my plan was a good one.

"We're here," I told Doug, putting the Hankies back in my pocket. The motor immediately slowed down.

At a snail's pace, we neared some vessels lit by torches. We came to a steop as the outline of a tiny, little island rose against the starry sky.

We had finally arrived at the fabled Island of the Passages.

A vessel drew up alongside ours without any of us noticing it. I turned and saw a man steering it with a long pole. The bottom of his boat was full of glass bottles that glittered beneath the stars.

"Who are you? I don't know you. You can't be here," the man said, drawing nearer until the sides of our two boats touched. Then he sniffed the air loudly and added, "I smell the rotten stench of Time on you. And I smell it very strongly."

He was a tall, imposing man. He had no hair and wasn't wearing a shirt. His half-naked body was decorated with a dense network of tattoos: letters, words, and complete phrases interspersed with spirals and question marks.

"My name is Finley McPhee — with an 'F,'" I said. "I was a friend of Cumai."

"I am Somerled," the green girl introduced herself. "And even though I am now called McBlack, I come from the Hollow World just like you and Cumai."

The man examined us morosely. His quiet boat bumped lightly into ours. "I heard your name, once," he said. Then he sniffed the air again and turned toward Doug. "So it's you who stinks so much of time. Do you have a coin to pay for your passage?"

"Hey, pal," Doug said through his teeth. "If there's someone who stinks here, it's —"

I interrupted him with a kick and passed him the two-headed coin I'd found at the bottom of the boat. "Show him your coin, Doug," I said.

"If you have a coin, smelly boy," the guardian with the pole continued, "now's the time to give it to me."

Doug tossed him the coin with a grunt. The Other examined it, then raised the pole and pushed his boat away from ours. "In any case, I advise you not to get off the boat, because the Others will smell you from miles away. And they aren't all nice and calm like me."

I nodded, unsure of what to say.

"Enjoy the show," the guardian said. With that, he disappeared into the darkness as silently as he'd arrived.

"Who the heck was that?" Doug asked.

"I think that was Wark," I said. "Cumai's brother."

"That was him, yes," Somerled agreed.

"That's no normal family, eh?" Doug grumbled, moving to start up the motor again.

"Wait," I said quietly. In the silence of night, I thought I'd heard something like the sound of a bottle being thrown into the sea. Then came the muffled buzz of crackling torches.

"Let's continue on with just our oars, Doug," I whispered. "I don't want them to notice our presence. At least not yet."

On the island beach, a very unusual group of people had gathered. On one side were villagers from Applecross, standing next to Piper's fishing boat. I recognized Mr. Everett, Reverend Prospero, Mr. McStay, and McBlack. In front of them was an alarming assembly of about twenty or so bizarre creatures. Several of them were carrying torches with dancing blue and orange flames. Several men were wearing long, colored overcoats and hats with antlers. I saw a few small and shimmering fairies. And there was one huge, furry being with big yellow eyes.

I also saw a man wearing an enormous sombrero and a skull-like grin. There was a very tall woman who

looked as transparent as a ghost, a giant with turquoise skin, and a person with the face of a cat peeking out from an ivory cape and cowl.

I also saw an armored knight with a broken sword, an extremely wise-looking wolf, and a little girl dressed in red who kept dropping her ball in the water.

And in the exact center of this amazing display was a woman with gray skin who looked like she'd been carved from a block of magnetite. She had a regal manner about her. Every time she spoke, the Others fell silent as if they were afraid of her every word. I imagined it had been her idea to take Reverend Prospero hostage.

Between the two groups rested a coffin covered by a red shroud that was embroidered with gold. Cumai had to be underneath it.

We waited.

When the two groups finished speaking, the Applecross residents left the beach to get back into the fishing boat. Reverend Prospero remained on the shore with the Others.

I gestured to Somerled. "The rest is up to us," I said. "Let's go."

WINDY HANKIES

Also known as Insincere Farewells, these
handkerchiefs of various colors and sizes have
always been sold in sets of twelve. When unfolded
and waved, they allow a sea traveler to move much
more swiftly — as long as the waving continues.

Chapter
TWENTY-ONE

DAWN,
MIDDAY, &
EVENING

I awoke at dawn, a mere three hours after my head had hit the pillow. I rearranged my room to hide the writing on the wall and prepared to leave before anyone else was up. Doug was shaken by the previous evening's outing and was still asleep. I left him a note reminding him to stop by the Emporium to pick up Aiby for the picnic. I also stole back the defender's key to the Enchanted Emporium that I'd officially surrendered to Doug a few hours earlier.

I went down to the kitchen, slipped a chocolate bar into my pocket, and spent ten minutes making breakfast for everybody else.

I left my Mom a little note telling her to have a nice day. Then I left.

I went to Dad's shop, swiped a lighter, and used it to melt several candles to create a soft block of wax. I rolled it between my fingers, very satisfied with my work. I wrapped it up in a damp cloth and shoved that into my backpack, silently marveling at how many things I could get done in a single day if I really knew what I wanted to do.

I went back to the house, retrieved my bike with the invisible seat, and pedaled away with Patches yipping at my heels.

I checked the time — 5:30 a.m. If Mr. Everett had been telling me the truth, at this moment Semueld Askell would be starting his morning run. With a little luck, I'd see him running along the shore in his ridiculous shorts and athletic shoes.

But I wasn't lucky. Semueld was nowhere to be seen. So I pedaled up to the campground, hid my bike near the entrance, and silently slipped into his tent.

"Feel free to pee here, Patches," I said. My dog tilted his head at me in confusion, but did as he was told.

Now inside, I was terrified by the idea that I might fall into one of Askell's traps or get devoured by a trunk. But everything went well. I didn't touch a single magical object and restricted myself to putting the Heart-eating

Box back in its place on the table — otherwise Askell wouldn't be able to throw it at me when he met me later that afternoon.

To avoid having it eventually eat me, I'd had to accept the idea of placing the four required ingredients inside it and suffering the consequences. It had been a painful decision, but I'd had to make it. There was no other choice.

I had to do everything very swiftly to minimize the chances that Askell would catch me there. I found the four keys, opened the sarcophagi, lit the lighter under the block of wax to soften it, and pressed the keys into it to make molds of them. Then I ran out of the tent with Patches scurrying between my legs.

Patches's collar was missing. "Where did you lose your tags, boy?" I scolded him with a smirk. His collar had belonged to his father. Like all his forebears, he was also named Patches.

"One thing left to do," I said to myself.

I walked over to the two cyclists' tent and left a chocolate bar next to the zippered entrance. I attached a note to the bar that read:

Be careful not to leave kids in bike carts tonight!
— The Management.

With that done, I left the campground, pedaling in the direction of the Enchanted Emporium. But after the second bend in the road, I realized I would be changing the course of events if I continued on to the Enchanted Emporium.

Instead, I changed course and returned to the village to talk to Meb. I found her getting ready to leave her shop, and she spoke to me again about the Holiday Suitcase and the phobo-sensitive glasses. But this time around, I asked her a new question.

"If someone stole one of the keys to the Emporium," I said, "and used it to go inside the shop . . . what do you think would happen?"

"They can't be stolen, not permanently," Meb said. "After a short time, the keys return on their own to their true owners."

"After how much time?" I asked.

"A day, I think," Meb said.

"But can the thief use the key in the meantime to enter the shop?" I asked.

Meb shrugged. "I vaguely recall Locan telling me about the Emporium's defense system," she said. "If I remember correctly, it will turn any intruder into a pillar of salt."

A huge smile stretched across my face. I hugged her. "Thanks, Meb!" I said. "That's exactly what I was hoping to hear!"

I slipped Patches into my backpack and made a mental note to remember not to enter Aiby's house without the key for any reason whatsoever.

The day continued exactly like the one I had lived through before. I interrupted Mr. Lily a few times during our conversation, just to be consistent. When Aiby informed me she'd lost the case for her Fludd Lenses, which had stayed in my backpack, I saw to it that she found it on the table outside. Aiby was somewhat surprised it was there, but she didn't ask any questions about it.

Then I asked her to help me make copies of the keys that I'd created the wax impressions of, lying that they were for my parents. Aiby handed them over to a little man, a so-called Keychain, who disappeared into Locan's workshop and came out a short while later with a handful of brand-new keys.

During the conversation, I was careful to stay on the porch in front of Locan Lily's Bubble of Silence beneath the strict watch of the seagulls. Shortly thereafter, the meeting with Somerled at the Black Birch went smoothly

209

since she skillfully feigned ignorance all the way to the end. When we got into the boat this time around, I didn't have to argue with Doug because I'd already warned him about everything. Well, *almost* everything.

Aiby and I climbed to the top of the Sheir Thraid tower. This time, when Aiby came so close to me that I could feel her breath on my face, I closed my eyes, put my hands in her hair, and gave her a kiss.

Just like that, I'd kissed her. A real kiss, ladies and gentlemen, as sure as my name is Finley McPhee. And the moment after, before my legs got too weak to do it, I dove into the waves and discovered for a second time that I was a Borderpasser.

When I surfaced in the water, Aiby was quiet and seemed simultaneously both happy and scared. It didn't seem like Doug had noticed anything, so I retrieved a Borderpassing coin from the sea.

We went to the mill. I opened the door to the entrance without hesitation, pretended to find the dart from the blowgun and the shard from the Cloak of Mirrors on the ground (which I actually had hidden in my backpack), and savored Doug's dumbfounded expression when he saw us literally disappear into a closet.

"Hey, Viper," Doug said to me when we reappeared. "What —"

"Let it be for now, Doug," I said. "I'll explain it to you this evening. And go open the door, please."

"The door?" he asked.

"Don't you hear footsteps outside?" I said.

When Mr. Everett arrived, he showed a little less surprise than the day before. This time he began to tell the story of the tree with blue leaves when we were still at the mill, instead of along the street like he had the previous day. We moved toward the campground, and I hoped that Somerled, in the meantime, had gone to talk to Mr. Lily as we'd agreed she should do. So far, everything I had planned had proceeded perfectly.

The rest of the day played out much like the day before. Doug and Aiby went into the tent, but I didn't voice any objections this time. I waited until they disappeared inside, waved to the tourists with the toddler in the bike cart, and then followed Mr. Everett inside.

Everything was exactly like the day before. But all of a sudden, instead of feeling reassured, everything became frightening to me. If I messed up this time, I wouldn't get another second chance.

Semueld Askell appeared in the tent. "I've been waiting for you, McPhee," he said, taking off his Cloak of Mirrors.

Shortly after, he tossed the box at me. I caught it, cleverly pretending that it bit me even though it really hadn't.

"To capture the heart of your loved one, McPhee, all you have to do is put four things inside," Semueld said. "Something from the body, something from the dead, something that's liquid, and something that's worn."

I pretended to be appalled, but I interrupted him before he could further explain about the ingredients. "I get it, I get it!" I said. "I'm in! You've convinced me."

He seemed perplexed. "In what sense did I persuade you?" he asked.

Everything depended on how I played my last scene. It had to be perfect. Semueld had to buy my performance.

I took a deep breath. "There must be something true about what you've told me," I said, "because it just so happens that I already have everything that's needed right here with me."

I slipped off my backpack. "Here's a handkerchief that Aiby dried her tears with. Here's a lock of her hair. Here's one of her shirts. And this half-broken clock once belonged to her mother."

"Ah," Askell murmured. "Her mother, of course."

"Now I just have to close it?" I asked.

"Exactly so," he replied.

"And you guarantee it will work?" I asked.

"Yes," he said.

I hesitated for a moment, pretending to weigh my options. Finally, I said, "Okay. Here's the key." I showed him the scorpion key that I'd retrieved from my brother's room after naming Doug the guardian of the Enchanted Emporium.

Askell narrowed his eyes as if he were trying to read my mind. Even if he could've, all he would've heard in my head was, "Do you want the scorpion key? Then take it already!"

"We truly live in a crazy world, don't we?" I said, mimicking the pretentious manner of speech he seemed so fond of.

Askell raised an eyebrow. "Truly crazy," he muttered. "You're a real surprise, McPhee. I was convinced the Lilys had chosen more wisely."

"Wisely in what way?" I asked.

"I didn't think you'd betray them so easily," Askell said, suspicion in his voice.

"But real men always betray," I said with a wink, quoting one of my brother's favorite (and incredibly tasteless) sayings.

It worked. Semueld Askell grinned broadly and nodded. "Exactly, McPhee. Exactly. Perhaps I was wrong about you."

"Perhaps," I said.

I extended the key with the scorpion on the handle out to Askell. He snatched it from my hand. In a heartbeat, Askell transformed into a flock of ravens and flew away.

Borderpassing Coins

BORDERPASSING COINS HAVE TWO HEADS AND
NO TAIL. THEY COME IN SEVERAL VARIETIES,
BUT ALL OF THEM HAVE THE FOLLOWING IN
COMMON: ONE SIDE DEPICTS THE HEAD OF A
MAN (TIME), AND THE OTHER SIDE DEPICTS
THE HEAD OF A WOMAN (MAGIC). THEY
ARE USED AS BARGAINING CHIPS WHENEVER
THERE IS A DISPUTE TO SETTLE, SAFE PASSAGE
TO GUARANTEE, OR A DELIVERY TO MAKE
BETWEEN THE TWO WORLDS.

No. 337,238.

ENCHANTED EMPORIUM

Fig.1.

Chapter
TWENTY-TWO

THE DEFENDER,
THE PILLAR OF SALT, &
THE TWO KINGS

This time I didn't chase the ravens. Instead, I stayed inside the tent and looked for the blowgun and its Sidhe darts. When I found it, I placed it into one of the Essential Pouches in my backpack. I did the same with Cumai's violin, scarf, and wand.

The backpack was getting pretty heavy. Thankfully, the tourists had taken their son out of the bike cart so I could steal it from them without any consequences.

Well, without any kidnapping-related consequences, anyway, I thought.

I pedaled to Meb's house at top speed. "Come on! Come on! Come on!" I repeated with every push on the pedals.

If the Others held to what they'd promised when Somerled and I had requested an audience on the Island of the Passages, then they'd be at the Enchanted Emporium waiting for the delivery.

Meanwhile, Somerled had done what she was supposed to. I found her at the dress shop with Meb and Mr. Lily.

"So?" They asked me as soon as I arrived. "How did it go?"

"I think it went well," I said honestly. "What about you two?"

"I'd say it went well for us, too," Somerled said. "Well, except that my father is still searching for me everywhere."

"And what about the Others?" I asked.

"They're waiting outside the Emporium, as agreed," Somerled said. "Were you able to get Cumai's items?"

I showed them the magical bags, one after the other. Patches sniffed each one carefully.

"Then all that's left is to free them," Mr. Lily said.

We got in Meb's car and raced to the village. We used the first of the four keys to free Mr. Everett from his trunk. He almost fainted in our arms, but we didn't have time to comfort him.

We sped to my farm, but there was no trace of Doug's trunk there. It felt like a bad premonition.

"Listen, Finley," Somerled said as Meb drove us to the Enchanted Emporium at top speed. "Is it possible that this evening, your brother heard part of your story in the boat and did something different from the first time?"

"I don't even want to consider that possibility," I said.

Meb parked her car on the main road right beneath the sign with the arrow that changed direction depending on where you stood.

Mr. Lily pulled two swords, a bow, and a crossbow out of the trunk of Meb's little car. "You never know what might end up being useful," Mr. Lily muttered. He gave Somerled the bow. He started to hand the crossbow to Meb, but changed his mind and kept it for himself. He handed Meb one of the swords, apologizing for not having healed enough to wield a sword.

We covered the rest of the journey on foot. Each step made me grow more and more wary.

"Do you want to know who these magical weapons belong to?" Locan asked as we crossed the remnants of the burned-down forest.

Patches replied with a low growl, which would've

been quite similar to my response. No one else responded to Mr Lily's question, so we traveled in silence until we reached the curve of the cliff.

I pointed out the raven and the seagull feathers that were scattered on the white stones.

"I'd say there was a battle here," Somerled said, picking up a couple of feathers.

Locan Lily loaded the crossbow and advanced slowly. Meb and Somerled flanked him. I took up the rear.

A trunk was resting on the ground in front of the Emporium's porch. I heard the sound of thumping and rushed toward it. Before I could get to it, I saw a few cranky seagulls flying over the house. Another, much more regal looking seagull was staring at us from the doorway to the store. As soon as the bird recognized Mr. Lily, it let out a sharp, harrowing call and limped over to us. It looked like a wounded general coming home from a hard-fought battle.

Locan Lily knelt down before it and stroked the seagull's feathers. The two seemed to be communicating somehow. "Askell's here," Mr. Lily said.

"Where?" I asked, looking around anxiously.

Mr. Lily pointed to the wide-open door of the Enchanted Emporium. Just then, the trunk vibrated with a second round of thumping.

"Get Aiby out, I beg you," Mr. Lily said, raising the crossbow so he could sight it. He proceeded one step at a time toward the entrance to the Enchanted Emporium.

Somerled followed, bow in hand, but with the arrow pointing at the ground.

I threw the keys to the trunks to Meb, raised my sword, and followed Mr. Lily and Somerled.

When Mr. Lily finally reached the door, his weapon was aimed at the unlit interior of the shop. I could barely see his pale, wild hair set against the darkness inside as he entered.

I gestured to Somerled to follow Mr. Lily. Behind us, I could hear keys jingling and Meb repeating the words, "Just a minute, Aiby! Just a minute!"

The darkness swallowed up Mr. Lily and Somerled. I could only hear their steps creaking softly inside.

"I found the key," Mr. Lily said from inside the shop. "Here."

After a long moment of silence, the scorpion key clinked on the ground at my feet. I grabbed it. The sound reminded me to breathe.

I heard a few more sounds come from inside Mr. Lily's lab, and then he was calling me. "Finley? Can you come help us?"

I gripped the key in my hand, feeling helpless. Since

the key was no longer mine, I was no longer the shop's defender. The Emporium wouldn't let me come inside. "I don't think I can do that, Mr. Lily," I called back. "At least not before I explain everything to your house."

At that point, Patches barked furiously. I spun around with a jerk. Meb had opened the trunk. Aiby hopped out and shouted "And wash those smelly feet of yours, Doug!"

And before I could figure out what was happening, I saw my brother jump out of the same trunk. "Listen, Aiby," he said with a shrug. "I'm really sorry, but once my feet start sweating, I can't make them stop!"

In a flash, I reconstructed what had happened. Somerled had been right: Doug must've overheard the part of my story where I'd explained that he and Aiby were going to get trapped in the trunks. Somehow, he'd managed to get stuck in the same one as her.

I snickered nervously. Judging from Aiby's wrath, my brother's attempt at getting close to Aiby had backfire. The mortified expression on my brother's face helped to calm me down.

(A few days later, Doug told me that being trapped inside the trunk with Aiby had been like sharing a small space with an angry tarantula. I didn't bother to ask for details.)

"Doug!" I said. I pointed at the entrance to the store and slyly slipped the key into his pocket when he turned to look. "Can you go inside and give Mr. Lily some backup?"

"He won't be angry with me, right?" Doug asked.

"No, don't worry. He didn't notice anything," I reassured him. "Go on, they need someone strong to help out."

Patches started barking wildly, and for good reason: the Others were coming. Their blue and orange torches flickered on the sea like an army of hovering glow-worms. Three boats were docking at the Reginald Bay wharf.

The floor of the Enchanted Emporium creaked. Doug cried out in terror as a salt statue of Semueld Askell rolled outside the store and landed at our feet.

"Ah!" my brother exclaimed. "Did I break that? What the heck is that thing?!"

I helped Doug place the statue back on its feet. We noticed that the fall had damaged its right ear. I tried to put it back in the place, but it wouldn't stick.

Askell's crystallized face was impressive. It reminded me of the woman made of stone I'd seen on the Island of the Passages. But this time, I wasn't frightened — I just couldn't believe that Semueld had been so confident

that he'd entered the Enchanted Emporium without any hesitation.

I patted the statue on the cheek. "I'm sorry about your ear," I said. "But I'm sure your friends will fix it for you soon."

Meb watched me with wide eyes, clearly dying to ask hundreds of questions.

Aiby kneeled next to me, slipped her fingers into mine, and squeezed them. "I have to talk to you," she whispered.

"Me, too," I whispered back.

"I need to tell you about the Ark of the Passages," she added.

"What do you need to tell me?" I asked.

"That maybe I didn't tell you the whole truth, exactly," she said.

"Me neither," I admitted.

But in any case, it wasn't the right time to explain. A small delegation of Others had come ashore. A man with long hair, exquisite clothing, and a sparkling crown led them toward us. Just behind him was the knight with a broken sword.

Reverend Prospero walked in the middle of the procession, his head high and his hands wrapped in a long silk scarf. Behind him walked a woman whose face seemed to be made of flames. Next to her was an ugly guy with a hook for a hand and the skeleton of a parrot dancing on his shoulder.

Cumai's brother, the guardian of the island of Fladda-chùain, stayed back on the boat. He was watching the bottom of the cliff with a grim look on his face. From time to time, he extended the pole to touch the shore, as if he wasn't allowed on the land.

The Others reached the Enchanted Emporium and waited silently. I didn't know whether to look at the woman with the flaming face or the man with the crown on his head. Both of them seemed equally terrifying and regal, like a king and queen born from the stuff of nightmares.

Mr. Lily stepped forward. He placed both his hands over his heart and then raised one hand, making the same gesture that I had seen Revered Prospero make at the end of the bonfire the day before. (Or two days before, depending on who's counting).

"Hail to thee, Oberon, King of the Little People," Mr. Lily announced. He performed a strange bow. "And hail to thee, Arthur Pendragon, son of Uther. We are honored by your visit."

"Hail to you, Locan Langmuir Lily and Aiby Agnes Lily," the man named Oberon bellowed. "It's been a long

225

time since I've passed through the Veil to meet you in this place."

"I beg you to drink a toast with us," Mr. Lily continued. "We have prepared cups of fresh milk and cream for you."

"I would do that with great pleasure, Locan Langmuir Lily, if the occasion that brought us to you were not so dire," said Oberon, the King of the Sidhe. He let his calm gaze pass over each of us, and then asked, "Therefore, please tell us which one of you is the guilty party you proclaimed you would surrender to us this night."

"The man of salt," Mr. Lily answered.

"And how can we be sure?" Oberon asked. "Can he speak to us?"

"Not now," Mr. Lily said. "Not for another seven nights, in fact. But we've gathered evidence against him that leaves no doubt of his guilt. In Cumai's mill, we found the tip of the dart that he used to dispel her mortality. We also found a fragment of his mirrored cloak on the premises."

Mr. Lily motioned for me to bring both objects to Oberon, which I did slowly and carefully. Oberon took the objects and examined them with interest, then passed them to the warrior next to him.

Mr. Lily held out the three objects I'd gathered earlier that day. "In the tent belonging to the man of salt, we found this violin, this scarf, and this wand," Mr. Lily said. "I believe that all of you will easily recognize them as Cumai's belongings."

The items passed from hand to hand. From the boat, Wark bellowed in grief.

"We recognize them," the King of the Sidhe confirmed. "And I thank you for returning them to us."

"You shouldn't thank me, but rather the other three people who help me take care of the Enchanted Emporium," Mr. Lily said. "You've met my daughter, Aiby Agnes, but you should also meet my repair person, Meb McCameron, and the shop's defender, young McPhee."

Meb curtsied. I pushed my brother forward. He gave a slight bow.

Aiby stared at me in stunned silence.

King Oberon scratched his beard. "So there is still honor among the shopkeepers," he said. "That is good news to bring to the rest of our people."

"We heard about your discontent," Mr. Lily said. "We have tried to behave in accordance with the ancient traditions."

Oberon waved his hand as if to change the subject.

Mr. Lily continued. "To speak the truth, I must inform you that the man we're surrendering to you is also a shopkeeper," he said. "He belongs to the Askell family, who will run the Emporium after my family's term has ended."

Oberon grunted. "So there *is* a good reason for our discontent," he said. "If even the shopkeepers are betraying the pact."

Arthur stepped forward. "Time keeps growing larger and opens up cracks in every heart," he said. "What pains me the most about Cumai's death is that perhaps we really will have to close all the passages soon."

Everyone present went silent, letting Arthur's melancholy words linger in the air. Then, as if rousing himself from an agonizing lethargy, Oberon turned toward Reverend Prospero and said, "But the agreements between us are clear, and they have been followed honorably. We shall honor the agreement and exchange the culprit for your priest!"

With a stroke of his broken sword, Arthur severed the silk scarf that bound Reverend Prospero's hands. Then he bowed. "It is not customary for a king to pay respect to his hostage," Arthur said, "but in this case, the Others were wrong about you, Reverend — and about your loyalty to your friends. We restore you to your beloved Time, and to those who wish you well."

Reverend Prospero answered the bow with a grunt and a decidedly stiffer bow. "I accept your words as if they were an apology, my Lords," he said. "And I leave your hospitality with great pleasure. Ladies, Sirs, I give you all my most sincere blessing —"

"Reverend, please," Oberon interrupted, placing a hand on Arthur's before the knight could raise his sword. "We've already discussed our differences about faith. I do not believe it's the right time to stir up our ancient rivalry this evening."

The Revered lowered his head and walked over to join us. Oberon then commanded the pirate to take the salt statue of Semueld Askell and carry it to the wharf, something the Other did without any apparent strain or effort (which Doug watched with obvious admiration).

King Oberon was the last to take his leave. "Thank you, Locan Langmuir Lily. Thank you, Aiby Agnes, Meb McCameron, and young McPhee. Reverend Prospero, we shall have an opportunity to continue our discussion next time, which — like you — I hope will be far into the future. And now we shall take our leave, accompanied by the night."

"Sire?" Somerled said, taking a step forward. "I have something to ask of you. I haven't been able to return home for four hundred years now. If there's room for me on one of your vessels, I would very much like to go with you."

Oberon's gaze was distant and filled with a sort of omnipotent disinterest. He pointed to the wharf and the vast sea beyond. "You may come with us," he said, "if that is what you truly desire."

And without another word, he left.

Somerled smiled at us, kissed us, and squeezed my hand between hers. Her hand trembling, she passed the Reverend a letter. "My adoptive father trusts your words greatly," she said to the Reverend. "Please tell him about this night as you think best and give him this."

"Of course, my child," the Reverend replied, kissing her on the top of her head. "Of course, child of the Lord."

SIDHE VIOLIN

(No Model.)

No. 425,390.

Fig. 2.

Patented Apr. 3, 1890.

This ancient Irish violin has strings made
of spider silk and a bow made from elytra,
the hardened front wings of beetles. It
can only be played by one of the Sidhe
(also known as the Others). The initials
W.H.G.F. are engraved inside it, which
probably refer to Sir Grattan Flood,
who admired it greatly. Its music
forces the Sidhe to dance until
the musician ceases playing.

W. H. G. F.

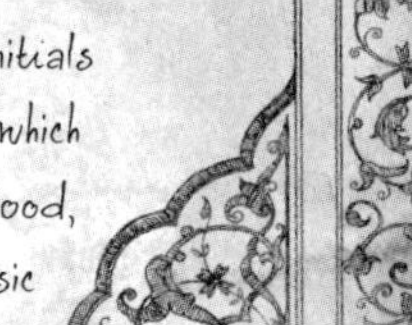

Mr GRATTAN FLOOD
No. 549,160.

THE
YOUNG HOLES&BROS
PATENT

Chapter
TWENTY-THREE

LOVE,
TRUST, &
JEALOUSY

I stared out at the islands on the bay, chewing a blade of grass. Aiby and I were sitting on the hill at the location of Cumai's funereal bonfire. The two of us had so many things to talk about, but we remained silent. We were exhausted — both physically and emotionally — and our heads were too preoccupied with the events of the previous day (which went double for me).

After the meeting with the Sidhe King and the other Others, I slept for twelve straight hours. When I finally woke up, I found my brother in the bathroom violently scrubbing his feet.

"Do you think they stink?" he asked in a small voice.

I didn't reply because I was furious at him. Doug had been unwilling to return the key to the Enchanted

Emporium to me. He claimed that I gave it to him as a gift — not because I was trying to trick Askell. He made it clear that I would never get it back, which made him the defender of the Enchanted Emporium.

"That may be a problem," was all Mr. Lily had said after I'd shared the news. Aiby had said nothing at all.

Patches was crouched nearby, enjoying the breeze rustling the fur between his ears. I had already told Aiby everything about how I'd used the Second Chance Watch to trick Semueld Askell into falling for the simplest of traps.

Mr. Lily and Meb had gone to the campground to dismantle the tent using the Holiday Suitcase that Meb had recently repaired. The tent and all its contents would be placed inside until it could be given directly to the Askells at the next meeting of the seven families.

But all those matters seemed very distant, like they were a part of a future that I couldn't yet be bothered imagine. In that moment, I only thought of the blade of grass between my teeth, the early afternoon breeze, and the presence of Aiby and Patches next to me.

"Can I ask you a question?" Aiby said, finally breaking the silence and pulling me out of my thoughts.

"Anything," I said.

Aiby was stretched out on her side, staring me right

in the eyes, her freckles highlighted in the sun. If I had been a ladybug, I would've hopped patiently from each irresistably cute freckle to the next.

"There's one part of your story I don't get," she said.

"Just one?" I said with a smirk. "You're lucky, then."

"Wise guy," Aiby said. She tried to grab my blade of grass, but I protected it with my palm. We wrestled for a little bit. It was a lovely battle.

Aiby resumed her reclined position in the grass. "What I don't understand is how you got the Heart-eating Box to close so you could leave it in Askell's tent."

"Oh," I said, flustered. "You see . . ." I trailed off.

"The only way to close it was to give it the four things it wanted," Aiby said. "Or it would've eaten you."

I flushed red. "Yeah."

"And you swore you didn't use it on me," Aiby said, almost a question. "So . . . ?"

I couldn't resist messing with her a little. "So you don't feel any differently now? About our friendship?"

"Finley!" Aiby snarled.

"And that kiss above the reef?" I said with a grin. "Wasn't it out of this world?"

Aiby crossed her arms. "I don't want to talk about that with you. Not a chance."

I smiled at her, which quickly soothed her agitation.

"In any case, you were brave," Aiby said."

"Brave?" I said.

"Yes. You were brave," she said.

I tilted my head. "You mean I was brave for jumping from the tower?"

"I meant what I meant," Aiby said. "And you understood it perfectly well."

But this time, I didn't understand, although I pretended that I did. "Okay," I said. "Then I'll tell you what happened with the box. On the condition that you don't tell anyone else."

Aiby stared me down. "Tell me."

I stared right back. "Promise you won't tell anyone."

Aiby nodded. "I promise I won't tell anyone."

"Okay," I said. "I didn't perform any Heart-eating voodoo ritual on you, but I had to do it to someone. The only way to stop that box from eating me whole was to put four items from someone else inside it."

Aiby narrowed her eyes. "And? What objects did you put inside the box?"

"Well, for something that's worn, I put his collar inside the box," I said. "For something from the dead, I used his dog tag — because it had belonged to his father, who's been dead for years. I placed a few hairs from his

236

tail inside, too. As for the liquid, well . . . I asked him to pee a little."

Aiby roared with laughter. "Oh, Finley! You hexed poor Patches?"

Hearing his name, Patches dashed over to drool on my face in complete contentedment. "Yep!" I said. "I figured there was no harm in it. He was already madly in love with me, anyway. And it seemed to work out well enough for all of us."

Aiby smiled at me and placed her hand on my shoulder — until Patches whimpered and nudged it away with his nose.

I smirked. "Okay, so maybe he's a little more jealous than before," I said. "But after all, that's love, isn't it?"

PIERDOMENICO BACCALARIO

I was born on March 6, 1974, in Acqui Terme, a small and beautiful town of Piedmont, Italy. I grew up with my three dogs, my black bicycle, and Andrea, a special girl who lived five miles uphill from my house.

During my boring high school classes, I often pretended to take notes while I actually wrote stories. Around that time, I also met a group of friends who were fans of role-playing games. Together, we invented and explored dozens of fantastic worlds. I was always a curious but quiet explorer.

While attending law school, I won an award for my novel, *The Road Warrior*. It was one of the most beautiful days of my entire life. From that moment on, I wrote and published my novels. After graduating, I worked in museums and regaled visitors with interesting stories about all the dusty, old objects housed within.

Soon after, I started traveling. I visited Celle Ligure, Pisa, Rome, Verona, London, and many other places. I've always loved seeing new places and discovering new cultures, even if I always end up back where I started.

There is one particular place that I love to visit: in the Susa Valley, there's a tree you can climb that will let you see the most magnificent landscape on the entire planet. If you don't mind long walks, I will gladly tell you how to get there . . . as long as you promise to keep it a secret.

Pierdomenico Baccalario

IACOPO BRUNO

I once had a very special friend who had everything he could possibly want. You see, ever since we were kids, he owned a magical pencil with two perfectly sharp ends. Whenever my friend wanted something, he drew it — and it came to life!

Once, he drew a spaceship — and we boarded it and went on a nice little tour around the galaxy.

Another time, he drew a sparkling red plane that was very similar to the Red Baron's, only a little smaller. He piloted us inside a giant volcano that had erupted only an hour earlier.

Whenever my friend was tired, he drew a big bed. We dreamed through the night until the morning light shone through the drawn shades.

This great friend of mine eventually moved to China . . . but he left his magic pencil with me!

TO OPEN, ASK
MR. FINLEY MCPHEE
OF APPLECROSS
(SCOTLAND)

FRAGILE
DO NOT DROP

TO OPEN,
ASK MR.
FINLEY MCPHEE
OF APPLECROSS
(SCOTLAND)

HANDLE WITH
3 CARE
contains
Mr. Douglas
McPhee

TO BE OPENED
PREFERABLY
BEFORE
MIDNIGHT

DELIVER TO
Name: *The McPhee Family*
Address: *Camusterrach*
City: *Applecross*
Country: *Scotland*

Hermetically sealed
STRANGE
SARCOPHAGI

Robt Stewart

135 & 137, High Street
ELGIN, N.B